More praise for
WORKING MURDER

"Boylan has created a terse, old-fashioned mystery, sprinkled with humor and urbanity in the manner of Christie."

Pittsburgh Post-Gazette

"A contemporary page turner with a 1940 feel.

Tulsa World

"Clara Gamadge is one of the most interesting of the recent spate of senior-citizen sleuths, and I look forward to her next case."

The Virginia-Pilot/The Ledger Star

"Well written, evocative of golden-age inter-familial rivalries and relationships, and neatly plotted."

Murder ad lib

"Genuinely moving. Boylan has the courage (and talent) to tell a small, classic whodunit, with warm characters and feeling. Many happy returns, Clara."

The Kirkus Reviews

Also by Eleanor Boylan
Published by Ivy Books:

MURDER OBSERVED
MURDER MACHREE

WORKING MURDER

Eleanor Boylan

1989
168p

IVY BOOKS • NEW YORK

Ivy Books
Published by Ballantine Books
Copyright © 1989 by Eleanor Boylan

Library of Congress Catalog Card Number: 88-26732

ISBN 0-8041-0813-7

This edition published by arrangement with Henry Holt and Company, Inc.

Printed in Canada

First Ballantine Books Edition: March 1992
Fourth Printing: January 1995

FOR ELIZABETH DALY,

beloved aunt and inspiration,
creator of Henry Gamadge

1

"CLARA? CLARA GAMADGE?"

The voice on the phone was high, Eleanor Roosevelty, unmistakable. I said: "Aunt May."

"You angel—you knew my voice. It's been ages."

"How are you?" I said. "*Where* are you?" Please God, not at the Sarasota airport

"In New York. Still at 740 Park. I'm miserable, Clara. Something horrid has happened. Your husband would have known just what to do. How you must miss that dear man!"

I did indeed sorely miss that dear man and his penchant for involving himself in other people's horrid happenings. But now I could only look longingly at my paintbox, which I'd been in the act of packing, along with a sandwich and a paperbook copy of *Middlemarch*. May was going on about her own widowhood, which, as it antedated mine by about twenty years, was not, I felt, a pressing matter for condolence. She ended accusingly:

"And you never said good-bye when you moved to Florida."

"I didn't move. I just leased my brownstone for a year. It was pretty empty after Henry died."

The Gulf of Mexico, fifty yards from where I stood,

was a preposterous shade of blue-green in the January sun. May said hastily:

"Oh, of course. But—a *year*? Isn't Florida sort of . . ." Her voice trailed.

I laughed. "Boring, banal, and bourgeois? The Three B's, Cousin Sadd calls them. What's the horrid thing that's happened, May?"

"Oh, it's too nasty. Let me get a cigarette."

Was this woman still smoking and alive? She'd been a daily two- or three-packer in her youth, and May Dawson had to be in her late eighties now, a good twenty years older than I. Never intimate or even congenial, we'd always been friendly. I reached for a hairbrush and tackled my long white hair, which my daughter won't allow me to cut. May's phone clunked around on some surface, and she was back. She coughed rackingly for a moment, made an attempt to speak, coughed again, and finally said:

"I'm still in bed. What time is it? I'm simply too depressed to drag my clothes on. You remember Lloyd Cavanaugh, that cousin on the Saddlier side. Well, he died yesterday and refuses to be buried."

I took in this unlikely sequence as I tried to pin up my hair with one hand and watched another cousin, Charles Saddlier by name, but "Sadd" for as long as I could remember, walk up the path with the *Times* under his arm. I hoped this particular cousin would be spared a while longer to make the world safe for curmudgeonry.

"What I mean is"—May coughed again and I shuddered—"there's that hideous mausoleum sitting in Holy Martyrs Cemetery with all those empty crypts that none of us wants to be buried in and you can't blame us but Lloyd is penniless and should be grateful and instead

2

he's left instructions that he be buried someplace in Ohio where he was born.''

I wondered what was so horrid about that, as May paused for breath.

"And here's the horrid part: I thought I'd persuaded his wife—what's her name—Helen—to have Lloyd buried in Holy Martyrs, and last week when he was sinking I even made that awful trip out to Queens to ask about opening the vault, and what did they tell me in the office? Somebody has been snooping around asking questions about the *stories*. That wretched place. We'll never live it down.''

The Dawson mausoleum. I'd seen pictures of it as a child and could perfectly envision the enormous marble structure dwarfing everything around it in old Holy Martyrs Cemetery in Queens, New York.

I said: "I remember there was supposed to be something scandalous about the place, but I was never told what it was. Sounds rather fascinating.''

May's high voice went higher. "You're safely in Florida and your name is Gamadge now. *You* won't have to face some lurid piece in one of those loathsome tabloids.''

I felt sudden pity. A long-ago, high-profile tragedy in May's family had rendered her pathologically sensitive to notoriety. This I understood and respected. But the Dawsons in general have been a snobbish, ingrown group to whom a breath of scandal is to be dreaded more than sin. My husband used to say that their motto was the same as the Scarlet Pimpernel's in his effete disguise: What's worse than a crime?—a blunder! I am the only Dawson who affectionately remembers an old family embarrassment involving a senile uncle whom I adored, for in the course of it I met Henry Gamadge, and my days as an inept, lonely little debutante were

3

over. Happiness, a sage once said, is not something you experience, it is something you remember. . . .

"May," I said, fighting memories and hoping I sounded ineffectual, "what can I do?"

"You can come."

"Come?"

"Come help us persuade Helen Cavanaugh to have Lloyd buried in the mausoleum. We'll all show up at Holy Martyrs, and the place will be opened—it hasn't been since that awful creature was buried there—and maybe those *stories*"—May seemed to put the word in italics each time she said it—"will evaporate. And aren't you staying with Sadd? Tell him to come too."

I said despairingly: "Will you hold on a minute, May? Sadd just came in."

"Of course." She coughed again. "I'll hold on."

Not for long you won't, I thought grimly. Sadd had seated himself on the porch (I can't bring myself to use the ersatz-elegant "Florida Room") and had folded the *Times* into quarters, a habit that dated back to his commuting days on the New York, New Haven and Hartford. He pushed his glasses up to a nesting place in his thick white hair and said:

"Lloyd Cavanaugh died in Hollis, New York." He pulled the glasses down again and squinted at the fine print of the obituary. " 'Son of Kenneth and Rose.' Why can't they get these things right? Her name was Rosamond. Anyway, it's nice to be so far away that you don't have to even debate about going to the funeral. Who was on the phone?"

"*Is* on the phone. May Dawson. She wants us to come to New York for that funeral we don't even have to debate about."

He stared at me. "She's out of her mind."

"It seems"—I don't know if I was angry or just

4

bored—"that there's some problem about getting Lloyd buried—or not buried—in that mausoleum, and somebody's dug up the rumors about the place and May believes that if we just show up en masse . . ." I went on to describe the salubrious effects of committing Lloyd's reluctant remains to Holy Martyrs Cemetery.

Sadd said: "She's right."

This family! "Then go, Sadd. But I have no intention of making a round trip to New York City in the middle of January, especially since I'm going home in April anyway—"

"You are not."

"—when the lease is up. So you tell May you'll be glad to come and you'll look forward to that nice, leisurely layover in Atlanta and the balmy weather in New York, and you'll be happy to browbeat Lloyd's widow, who has a perfect right to bury her husband wherever she—"

"Hello, May, this is Sadd." He had struggled to his short legs and reached the phone. "I agree it would be unfortunate to revive that sordid mausoleum story, but isn't there enough of the family up there for your purpose?" He was motioning to me to pick up on the kitchen extension. "You don't want to drag two tired, elderly people . . ."

When Sadd didn't want to do something he was "tired and elderly." At all other times he was "spry as a cricket, thank you," and he was. I walked reluctantly into the kitchen, where a fiery hibiscus was brushing the screen, closed my eyes, and took the receiver from the wall. May's voice was quavering on.

"—some person who was at a funeral near the mausoleum and saw the name DAWSON—you know the size of those letters over the door—and remembered the *stories* [italics again] and began to ask questions—"

"May," I had a sudden inspiration. "Why can't young Henry represent Sadd and me? He lives in Brooklyn Heights—I'll give you his phone number." I warmed as I thought of my son. He was the exact age, thirty-eight, that his father had been when I met him, and he was a clone of his dad, same gray eyes, mousy hair, good mind, and bad posture. "I'm sure he'll go, May, and he'll take his wife—you'll love Bettina—and anybody else he can muster. He's a dear thing—"

"He is indeed!" May's voice was suddenly gentle. "And he's standing right here. I'll put him on."

Sadd and I stared at each other across the kitchen aperture. What *was* this?

"Hello, Mother! Sadd, you there? Now, listen, you guys, be good eggs and haul ass up here."

Sadd said: "Henry, don't be vulgar." I was used to it.

"By the way, Mom, little Hen has been reading my old Oz books, and he needs you to reassure him about the Yoop."

I froze. Sadd was beginning to huff and puff, but I scarcely heard him. When Henry was a child we had a code: If you are away from home and something happens to upset or frighten you and you can't speak freely on the phone, refer to the Yoop, the man-eating giant in his favorite Oz book. Once when he was in boarding school, the Yoop had saved Henry from the torments of a bully; one summer when he was unhappy during a visit to friends in Maine, the Yoop had effected a summons home.

I said, as quietly as I could: "Henry, are you telling us there's trouble and you can't talk?"

"That's right, Mom. The good old Yoop."

My heart was thumping. Sadd said: "Can you call us later?"

"Well, no. So hop a plane tomorrow. There's an Eastern flight gets into LaGuardia at noon—I just checked. I can't meet you but I'll buy you a cab right here to May's. And bring warm stuff—it's snowing."

His receiver clicked. We stood still, ours in midair.

Sadd said, in an apocalyptic tone: "Snowing . . ."

He walked to the bookcase, which doubled as his wine chest, and took out a bottle of sherry. "Our elevenses today are going to be tenses. I assume that 'Yoop' business was a code?"

I nodded and sat down in a chair that had stood by the window of our living room on East Sixty-third Street. It was a straight-backed thing with carved arms, out of place in these airy surroundings, but I had brought it with me to cherish the memory of Henry Gamadge, so often stretched in it and puzzling over a horrid happening.

2

IT BEGAN, BEFORE I KNEW HIM, IN THE SUM-
mer of 1936.

Henry Gamadge, a modest, endearing man, scholar,
bibliophile, expert (he hated the word) discerner of
forged manuscripts, found himself in the midst of murder in a Maine resort. Almost apologetically he named
the killer, then fled back to his bachelor quarters on
East Sixty-third Street. But the low-profile, moneyed,
bookish society of New York now had him in its genteel
clutches, and Henry Gamadge became the man to consult about that most delectable phenomenon—scandal
and murder in "a good family."

When he died, people said to me (knowing I had
"helped")—"Clara, you will of course carry on for
Henry."

At first the thought had distressed—even repelled me.
I'd loved working with the manuscripts, but "detect-
ing" was another matter and without Henry, unthink-
able. Would I have the heart, the skill? The dangers in
which he involved himself often filled me with terror,
but I had to confess that his absorption, when a puzzle
presented itself, filled me with admiration—almost
envy. He once said that the first intimations of a mystery, the first faint stirrings of a question, were almost
as exciting as the answer.

I'd felt such intimations with my son's cryptic summons, felt the first faint stirrings. . . . And for the past year, the only mystery in my life had been how I was to go on living without Henry Gamadge.

About a month after he died—it was the bitterly cold November of 1988—a letter appeared in my mailbox with a Florida postmark and addressed in a familiar, appallingly bad handwriting. The mail was late that day owing to the icy condition of the sidewalks, and it was past four o'clock when I went back through the basement foyer of our brownstone carrying the usual load of catalogues and condolence letters. The former were boring, the latter heartbreaking. How many persons had Henry Gamadge helped, unknown even to me? The door of his workroom with all his beloved apparatus stood open, and his elderly, beautiful Siamese cat lay curled in the chair.

I said: "Loki, maybe you can bear this room, but I can't—not yet." I picked him up and went out, closing the door. We took the little elevator to the first floor, where Loki struggled out of my arms and stood dejectedly in the middle of the living room. I walked through it and on into the small front bedroom where my two-year-old granddaughter was napping, spread-eagle. I rearranged her and pushed a chair against the bed. How quiet the place was. I wished she'd wake up and bawl or that her mother would come back. I went into the kitchen, made myself a drink, took it back to the fireplace where there was no fire, and sat down.

The letter, deciphered, read:

Dear Favorite Cousin Clara:

I know, I know, you wish I'd type this.

But I'm sitting in a deck chair outside and the typewriter is in the house. If the glare gets too much—

we're in the eighties here—I'll have to go in and get my sunglasses and then maybe I'll type the whole thing over but I doubt it.

Now, don't argue with me—just come down here. You know you're miserable and you won't feel any better staying in that bloody cold canyon. And stop saying to yourself "but he used to love New York." Of course I did when I had youth and money (the two requirements for being happy there) but now I have none of the first and less of the second and while Florida is, in many respects, boring, banal, and bourgeois, certain aspects of it are so enormously appealing that if one can just get one's northeast nose out of the air long enough to try the place, one can begin to enjoy what amounts to life on another planet.

By the way, I don't mean just come for a visit; come live here—with me if you like. At least try it for a year. Put a tenant in there and *come*.

We've been out of touch, damn it, and the dear note you wrote me about my dumb flowers when Henry died brought you to "the eyes of my mind" as a Jamaican cook of ours used to say. So here's the Sadd story—pun intended.

As you know I came down here about three years ago right after Harriet died wanting only to escape the New York winter. I'd just sold my publishing house—I've probably told you all this on Christmas cards but here's something new: I've bought a three-bedroom house on a small island called Santa Martina. It's a countrified little spit mercifully free from the chic which infests so many of Florida's west coast barrier islands. Now, how to "sell" you?

Well, the climate is sublime for six months of the year, perfectly tolerable for three, and ghastly during July, August, and September. Then you can always

10

shoot back up north, or any other time for that matter, if you can't stand it or if you miss the kids, which I do not. Jon took all the money his mother left him and blew it on some hopeless, failed, off-Broadway opera and is now broke and sulking. Kathy's husband is a dreary money-grubber and their children are spoiled and unattractive; they live, thank heaven, in the far reaches of Toronto. So much for my image as a benign parent and/or grandparent.

My house would lend itself beautifully to a permanent guest and you and I always hit it off as young people. I cook for myself. Sometimes I drink too much but you'll never know it when I do and I'm not a slob. No problem, of course, about having your own quarters. The only thing we'd have to share is the sunset which takes place over the Gulf of Mexico and is often too much to watch alone.

You could pay something if you like but I don't need it. I bought this place as an investment and plan to move into a retirement home the minute I know I'm getting too gimp or nutty. So far I'm amazingly fit for seventy-four (aren't you some years younger?) and I walk a mile of beach every day. By the way, I've become a dedicated environmentalist and an article of mine called "Violating Our Shores" appeared in . . .

The baby awoke with a wail at that instant, and I had just dragged off her sopping diaper and carried her into the living room when her mother, my pretty daughter, Paula, came through the door, snow-covered, laughing, laden with bundles.

I said, swapping baby for bundles: "You look like Nora making her first entrance in *A Doll's House*."

"Nora would feel right at home out there." Paula

blew on her fingers. "Norway couldn't be colder. Well, I've had my last shopping spree. But I worry about you being alone when I go home tomorrow." Paula lived in Boston.

"I may go to Florida."

"Super! When did you decide? For how long?"

"I'm not sure. I'd stay with Cousin Sadd." I handed her the letter. "Does it sound crazy?"

"It sounds great!"

And it had been. Within weeks of that day a delightful young Belgian couple, on exchange from the University of Louvain, took up temporary residence on East Sixty-third Street; Loki did the same in Brooklyn Heights, and I on Santa Martina Island.

Sadd was right. We hit it off beautifully, probably because we at once established rules that allowed for separate interests and for days when our paths scarcely crossed at all. Sadd was absorbed in expanding his environmental article into a book, and I was able, for the first time in my life, to paint—and fully enjoy it. In the high-powered, critical atmosphere of New York I had been, since girlhood, timid to the point of inhibited about exposing my limitations, for I am solidly second—no, third rate. But in the indulgent ambiance of Florida, where at every jetty and cove one beholds an elderly dauber, I worked happily. Sadd kindly never commented on my efforts except for an occasional "that's pretty." In addition, at a painting class I met some pleasant people who play bridge, a game I enjoy and Sadd detests. He loves birding; I am bored by it and asked him not to describe every contour of feather or bill he'd observed while crouched in some swamp aggravating his arthritis. Sadd in turn extracted a promise that I never report anything adorable my grandchildren had said or done.

So our paths were healthily divergent, and we'd avoided asking each other how we thought it was "working out," though Sadd came close one day when he quoted Wilfrid Sheed: "Have you ever noticed that the first one to say 'aren't we having fun' spoils the fun?"

But the fun had been spoiled for Sadd—even shattered—by May's phone call and young Henry's baffling involvement which, Sadd said, had "revved" me unnecessarily.

I said: "I thought you never used slang. But 'rev' is wonderfully expressive, isn't it?"

"Don't change the subject. I thought 'nothing would induce you to make a round trip to New York in the middle of January.' "

"I thought so too till Henry came on."

We were sitting in deck chairs flooded by the sunset glow. The gulf breeze was a kiss and the sky pure Maxfield Parrish, but, unhappily, mood paints the scene and Sadd's was foul. He refilled his glass from the pitcher of martinis and said:

"Of course, if one is at the beck and call of one's children—"

"I am not at the 'beck and call' of anyone," I snapped. "I'm going because my son, who is not an alarmist, has urgently requested it." I refilled my own glass and reached for a cracker. "And speaking of requests, did you make that plane reservation for me?"

"Yes. The flight Henry suggested. We leave at nine-fifty."

"*We?*" In my surprise I dropped the cracker, and a gull swooped.

"If I let you go up there alone you won't come back."

13

I was very touched. I knew Sadd had been fretting about the approaching end of my stay, and I wanted him to know how thoroughly I'd enjoyed it.

"Sadd," I touched his arm, "not only will I come back, I'm fishing right now for an invitation for next winter."

"I suppose you realize"—he dropped ice into his glass—"that I have nothing warmer than a raincoat and will probably get pneumonia."

"Henry has all his father's things. You shall have his overcoat."

"Thank you. It should reach to my ankles. The Oliver Twist look. Why do you suppose Henry couldn't call us back?"

"I don't know. It bothers me. And what on earth was he doing at May's? To my knowledge he hasn't seen her in years."

We were silent for a while, Sadd no doubt thinking of May, as I was, with the deep pity her rather trying image always evoked. A snowy egret paced up and surveyed the plate of crackers. His beautiful long neck caught a pink glow from the sky as he arched for the crumbs I tossed. Sadd said:

"Just getting Lloyd buried in the mausoleum is apparently not the entire problem. There's something else—something perhaps quite unrelated."

Oh, wasn't it always something "quite unrelated," and how often it had started with a relatively innocent request like May's. Déjà vu was strong upon me. . . . "Clara, we want you and Henry for bridge tonight and while you're here perhaps Henry can look at some old letters we found in the attic. . . ." "Henry, you remember great-grandfather's collection of aquatints? Well, one of them seems to be missing. . . ." "Clara, we wish Henry would come and talk sense to poor old

14

Uncle—he's convinced the cleaning woman is Moll Flanders reincarnated. . . ."

Then, too often, horror and death.

I stood up. "Henry must be staying at May's tonight. That's why he couldn't call us back."

"Why not call Tina at home?" said Sadd.

Now, why hadn't I thought of that? I swallowed my drink, went into the house, and called my son's number in Brooklyn. A voice shouted "Yez? Hollow?" in an unidentifiable accent, then managed to convey that Mr. and Mrs. Gamadge and their little boy had all gone to see a relative in "Monhatting."

I hung up and turned to find that Sadd had followed me in.

"Good God, Sadd, they've *all* piled over to May's. What on earth . . . ?"

"One can only assume"—Sadd walked into the kitchen and opened the refrigerator—"that May invited them. Or sent for them—or whatever. Does she know Tina?"

"I don't think so." I sat down in the "horrid happening" chair and dug in my memory. "I don't think she even came to their wedding. She did send them a nice check, I remember." I dug further. "Years ago when she and Frank moved to New York after the—the awfulness—Henry and I used to take the children to visit them once in a while. May wasn't going anywhere much even then. How long since you've seen her?"

"Years."

"After Frank died she practically became a recluse. Who can blame her? I'm sure that business would have turned me into a zombie."

"Me too."

Frank and May Dawson's only child, a girl of eighteen, had disappeared from her prep school graduation

15

party at the Eastern Shores Yacht Club in Gloucester, Massachusetts, never to be seen or heard of again. The year was 1939.

Sadd came out of the kitchen eating a sandwich. "Of the hundreds of thousands of words written about the case, these have stayed with me—verbatim: 'Into oblivion she went, white prom dress fluttering.' " He stared out at the Gulf. "How much of it do you remember?"

"Not much. I was too young and dumb and selfish."

"I doubt the last two."

Oh, but yes. When one is twenty and in love, one is insulated by happiness. A cousin I scarcely knew had disappeared; there was a war brewing in Europe. Both facts had equal impact upon me—slight. I was to be married and that was the central fact of the universe.

I said: "It's remote, but do you suppose this mystifying business has anything to do with—what was her name?"

"Ellen. It's been fifty years though."

Sadd picked up the *Times* and looked at Lloyd Cavanaugh's obituary again. "Nice guy. Quite a gifted musician."

"Yes. Henry and I once went to a concert in that downtown church where he played the organ. May says he was 'penniless.' Was he?"

"May thinks anybody who isn't rich is penniless. Lloyd did have a big family, and I guess it was pretty slim pickings in that choir loft all those years." He tossed the newspaper into the wastebasket. "Who'd have thought his death would have opened such a can of worms? That blasted mausoleum. May's right—we'll never live it down. Shall I make you a sandwich?"

"No, thanks. Fill me in on that mausoleum story. All my life I've heard bits and scraps about some disreputable person who's buried there. Who is it?"

"James Cavanaugh."

"Who was he? Why disreputable?"

"I'll tell you on the plane tomorrow." Sadd was making himself another drink. "It's a sordid story, and if I talk about it now I'll probably get drunk. I'm going to bed. Damn it, I don't even have an alarm clock."

"I do."

3

"HE WAS A BOOTLEGGER AND, INDIRECTLY of course, a murderer. His own wife died of his rotten booze, as did countless other people. May I have more coffee, please?"

The flight attendant, a smiling woman not a whole lot younger than I (refreshing!), filled Sadd's cup. I was relieved he wasn't having a third Bloody Mary. It had taken us two stiff ones to get through the stupefying layover in Atlanta, and we were now ten minutes out of LaGuardia. I'd had him talking before that, but now Sadd was morose. He hated flying; hated the moth-eaten cap and scarf he'd unearthed for the trip; hated the child across the aisle whose wind-up helicopter kept spinning into our laps; hated the word "finalize," which the pilot had just used over the loudspeaker.

"There's no such word," growled Sadd. "You 'make final,' you don't 'finalize.' Damn garbage words they use."

I said, still trying to fill in the gaps of the story:

"So Jim Cavanaugh married Maura Dever in 1918 during a trip back to Ireland with his mother."

"His 'sainted' mother. All Irish crooks have 'sainted' mothers."

I remembered a picture of this bride in an album. "Wasn't Maura very pretty?"

18

"She was very beautiful."

"Why would she marry such a creature?"

Sadd shrugged. "A chance to come to this country? And Jim may have been handsome or dashing. Also, remember that some of his more charming traits might not have surfaced till Prohibition. That was a fertile ground for a lot of vices people didn't even know they had."

"And when Sainted Mother died he built that mausoleum in Holy Martyrs Cemetery."

"Yes, but he really built it for himself."

"Then why"—this had always baffled me—"did the name Dawson go on it and not Cavanaugh?"

Sadd smiled. "There isn't a spiteful bone in your body, Clara, so you probably won't comprehend this. Jim's brother, Martin by name, had, as the expression goes, 'bettered himself' by graduating from law school. He then further bettered himself, if you'll allow me to say so, by marrying Sara Saddlier, May's sister. Sara was the beauty of the family and her brother Will, my father, claimed she 'threw herself away.' Unfortunate expression—and not true, as it transpired."

Voices discussing this marriage echoed in my head from across the years.

Sadd went on: "May had just married a wealthy WASP, your uncle Frank Dawson, and they undoubtedly snubbed the Irish Catholic Cavanaughs. Jim, it seems, never forgave them. He knew that Holy Martyrs Cemetery in Queens was the last place on earth any Dawson would want to be buried. So he had their name emblazoned on the mausoleum. His pretext, we were told, was that he was magnanimously providing a resting place for the whole family and using their more distinguished name rather than his own humble one. Brother Martin was mortified, but what could he do?"

19

I couldn't help laughing. "You have to admit, Jim was ingenious as well as spiteful."

"Oh, very. But just *how* spiteful even he couldn't know, because he had to die himself to really set them up. Damn, my ears are killing me. Are we coming down?"

I said loudly, over seatbelt instructions: "You mean the rumors about the place being haunted or something?"

"Haunted? Where did you get that old-fashioned scenario? That isn't the rumor."

I said dutifully: "Then what is?"

Sadd snapped his seatbelt. "You know, I suppose, that Jim Cavanaugh is buried in that mausoleum alone?"

Alone? No, I hadn't known that. *Alone?*

"There are twelve crypts in the place, and he's the only one in there."

Snow was beating thickly against the window beside me as the plane sank and sank toward the earth. I envisioned whiteness enveloping the great pile of marble with its single occupant . . . about which someone had recently been asking questions. . . .

I said: "There must have been Cavanaugh relatives who wouldn't have minded being buried in Holy Martyrs."

"Oh, there were. Plenty. But not with Jim. Everywhere but with Jim. Nobody wanted to be buried with that viper."

"Sainted Mother is."

"Not even her." The plane bumped twice and we were down. "Martin had her removed and buried in his plot in Woodlawn."

"What about Jim's wife—the beautiful Maura?"

20

"Oh, she'd left him. She went back to Ireland when the booze started to get to her and died there."

"Then what *are* the rumors?"

In my exasperation I spoke too loudly. Heads turned as passengers jammed the aisles, and a plaintive, amplified voice begged them not to yet. Sadd said in my ear:

"That Jim Cavanaugh had used some of the crypts to house the remains of enemies."

"Enemies?" I was trying to take all this in. "Did he have so many?"

"Oh, come on, Clara, does a dog have fleas? Jim was a bootleg czar—remember?"

"Mother!"

It was too good to be true. Henry, who'd said he couldn't meet us, was waving from across the sea of heads at the baggage turntable.

I said: "Thank God. Things can't be too bad if he was able to get away."

Sadd said, winking at me: "There's a burr attached to my leg, and it's wearing a red hat and a pair of wet mittens which are soaking me. Please detach it."

"Darling!" I picked up little Hen and hugged him. "You won't find Gran complaining about wet mittens. Hug me tight!"

"I'm six and a half now." His damp embrace was heavenly. "I have a lot of new riddles. What do you call two banana skins lying on the floor?"

"I give up. Quick—there's my bag—grab it!"

"A pair of slippers!" yelled Hen, diving onto the conveyor.

"And there's my bag," said Sadd. "After it! Hello, Henry."

21

I turned to find my son behind me and reached my arms up to him. Why was he shaking?

"Mom, Sadd, I have ghastly news: May's dead."

I think Sadd took it in before I did. I remember seeing his Florida tan turn sort of beigy. Then I remember feeling a pain in my big toe. Hen had dropped a suitcase on it and was saying: "Do you give up, Gran?"

"Give what up, dear?" I was able to say.

"Why do baby elephants never eat breakfast?"

To this hour I don't know why baby elephants never eat breakfast, for my son hoisted the child in his arm and said:

"Hold the riddles, Hen. We'll go get the car, and Gran and Cousin Sadd will wait for us outside." He looked from Sadd to me, his face stricken. "I'm sorry to hit you with it like that, but I couldn't bear any chit-chat. You had to know quick."

Sadd said: "Before you go—how?"

"She took an overdose of sleep stuff last night. Have you got all your baggage?"

"Not possible," I heard myself say, then realizing they were both staring at me, I amended it: "Not possibly—I'm sure there's one more."

Henry made a move toward the turntable as Hen said: "What is the difference between an alligator and a—"

"Get the car, Henry," said Sadd. "We'll collect it all and meet you outside."

"Look for the red Datsun. I might be a few minutes. The snow's getting worse"

Henry swung his son onto his shoulders, and they disappeared in the crowd. I stood still, feeling Sadd's eyes boring into me. He looked like an aggravated troll glaring out from between his bedraggled cap and scarf. I might have smiled except that I was feeling a little sick. People pushed and shoved around us.

22

Sadd said: "And pray, what does *that* mean?"

"What does what mean? Let's move. I need air."

"And that mythical other bag we're waiting for?"

"Is mythical."

"So 'not possible' means May's overdose?"

"Of course it does." We were making our way through the throng. "I don't believe May wanted to die last night. Tonight or tomorrow night, maybe—I don't know what the poor thing's problem was—but last night, no. She was too anxious to see us."

"When you say she didn't 'want' to die, I assume you mean the overdose was accidental." Sadd's short legs were going like pistons trying to keep up with me. I tried to slow down but I was feeling distraught. "I don't know of an alternative, do you?"

"Of course I do, and so do you." I was wishing I'd kept my mouth shut. We'd arrived at the automatic doors, which kept opening to admit blasts of arctic air. I said: "Do you want to take turns going out there to watch for Henry?"

"I do not. Madam"—Sadd turned to a woman behind him—"would you mind removing your child from that spot unless you want to die of pneumonia, which I do not."

The poor woman dragged the child away, and I said, peering out through the white haze: "I suppose we can see him from here. I wish there weren't so many red cars—I keep getting my hopes up."

Sadd plucked the cap from his head, causing his hair literally to stand on end. He said:

"I have a new riddle for Hen: Why does anybody named Gamadge always suspect the sinister worst?"

"I give up," I said. "There's Henry."

4

"GRAN, DID YOU KNOW AUNT MAY WENT TO heaven?"

"Yes, dear."

Hen had eschewed the front seat and squeezed himself between Sadd and me in the back of the Datsun.

"What we would like to know"—Sadd removed Hen's potato chip-filled hand from his knee—"is whether anybody suspected she was planning on going."

We were approaching a slushy ramp to the Brooklyn-Queens Expressway. Henry flashed us an apologetic look in the rearview mirror. "I know you must both be in a fog about all this. I'll fill you in as soon as we get home. Tina will have lunch for us, and Hen goes to afternoon kindergarten."

"I go to school now," said Hen. "I can pigeon evens."

Sadd and I looked at each other blankly, and Henry said:

"I think we're trying for 'pledge allegiance.' You're probably both exhausted. After lunch I want you to take a rest. Then I'm afraid it's back out to Queens for Lloyd's wake."

I'd almost forgotten poor Lloyd.

Sadd said: "Lloyd's been rather upstaged by all this. By the way, what verified May's overdose?"

"A stomach check. And her doctor confirmed his prescription. No question it was suicide. She's at Campbell's. No visitation."

Sadd had flashed me a triumphant look but my only sensation at the moment was one of relief at the words "no visitation." Thank heaven. I was beginning to feel as they must have during the Great Plague—a death a day. Who had found poor May? I wondered. Sadd said:

"Are we still expected to railroad Lloyd into Holy Martyrs?"

"No." Henry slowed to a squishy crawl on the congested expressway. "Helen is definite about that. After the Mass tomorrow, he'll be flown to Ohio. She said it's what he wanted."

"Good for her. Damn!" Sadd massaged the side of his head. "That bloody pressure from the plane is still with me. And May? Shall we practice what she preached and open the spooky portals for her?"

Henry shrugged and said he guessed it was out of our hands.

"Her brother-in-law, what's his name—Tully—he's here for Lloyd's funeral, and he found poor May this morning—he says she goes to White Plains Memorial next to her husband."

"Wonderful!" Sadd chuckled. "The shunning continues. Jim Cavanaugh's curse prevails!"

I said: "Have you heard that bizarre story about the mausoleum, Henry?"

"Yes, May told me. Bizarre is right." The car swerved slightly but sickeningly. "God, it's slick as glass!"

"We shouldn't distract you," I said. "No more talking till we get home."

25

Sadd put his head back and closed his eyes.

Hen said: "Can I just *whisper* some riddles, Gran?"

"Of course, darling."

He and I began exchanging hushed riddles and "I-give-ups" while a name nagged me: Tully Hewitt. May's brother-in-law. He figured somewhere—somberly, I felt—in the tragedy of May's daughter, but how? The family oracle dozing beside me would know, but I hated to rouse him. When the familiar streets of Brooklyn Heights, elegant with snow, began to appear, I knew Sadd would have to come to anyway. I touched his hand and kept my voice low.

"Sadd, what do I connect Tully Hewitt with?"

His head jerked up and he looked at me with wide, staring eyes. I was contrite. "I'm sorry. I didn't realize you were so sound—"

"Not asleep at all. Just . . . groggy. This thing itches." He pulled the cap off his head. "Tully and his wife spent the summers next door to May and Frank in Gloucester. Their daughter disappeared from his house."

Of course. Tully and Irene Hewitt. Baffled . . . frantic . . . one day a pretty niece is a houseguest, the next she is off the map. Irene, May's sister, had died shortly afterward, never fully recovering from the shock.

Sadd said: "When Tully retired, he went up to live in Gloucester year-round. Nobody knows why he wants to stay in that big old ark of a house especially with Irene gone, but he won't budge."

Henry said, unexpectedly: "His garden there is his one interest in life."

How would Henry know that? I wondered briefly, then Hen said something like "there's the sachew of ribalry" and sure enough there she stood like a distant black pin across the snow-veiled water. Henry turned into Willow Street.

"Here we are. You must be starved."

"I could use a drink," said Sadd.

I said: "Henry, did May's problem have anything to do with a certain disappearance years ago?"

"It had everything to do with it."

Sadd and I looked at each other with the proverbial "wild surmise," and at that instant, Hen requested a transfer to the front seat so he could be "first out." A boot-waving hoist followed, and Henry stopped before what he and Tina always called Nice Ugly, a high, narrow old home of no particular style. Hen leaped out of the car and scrambled up the snow-covered stairs to where his petite, bright-eyed mother stood waving, a parka clutched around her shoulders.

Henry said: "Be careful of the curb—there's a foot of slush. I'll get the bags."

He opened the rear of the car, admitting waftings of snow in upon us. Sadd swore softly and pulled his cap back on. He said:

"Henry, go in and get out the bourbon. I'll see that your mother makes it without breaking her hip."

"*My* hip!" I snorted.

Henry took the buried steps two at a time. Sadd and I struggled out of the car in the graceful way that persons our age do, muttering imprecations against advancing years, small automobiles, and the inexcusability of the weather.

"First time I've seen my breath in three years," said Sadd. "Appalling sight."

Henry had reappeared with a broom and was sweeping a path up the stairs near the iron railing. He called: "Hang on here. It's safer than any human help."

Sadd and I began a hand-over-hand clutch of the railing like a pair of superannuated mountaineers. I thought of the beach where two days ago I had napped, the firm, warm sand better than any mattress.

I said: "This is absurd."

Sadd said: "This is obscene." Then he added: "And for heaven's sake, don't say anything about what you suspect."

"I don't suspect anything. I know."

Tina was out again, stretching her arms to us. "You two are good sports!" She grasped my hand, Henry grasped Sadd's, and they lugged us over the top step and into the house.

Inside, Nice Ugly was merely nice and not at all ugly. I'd always liked the way their renovations had opened up the rooms, preserved useful antiquities such as the pantry, and revealed a fireplace in which a heavenly blaze now crackled. Within minutes we were divested of our coats; I was mercifully shown to the bathroom, then to the kitchen, and introduced by Tina to a smiling Puerto Rican woman—"Teresita, a recent joy of my life!"—who was ladling out soup for Hen. He immediately said: "Gran, what's the difference between a giraffe with mumps and a—" but the soup cut him off, and his mother and I fled down the hall.

"He's riddle-mad since you gave him that book for Christmas." Tina hugged me. "It's awful to drag you up here for this, but I *am* so glad to see you!"

How pretty she looked in a red skirt and white sweater, her long, black hair very shiny. Tina and I were old friends. I'd known her before my son did— had, in fact, introduced them. She was a "lady lawyer" (she teased me about the reactionary term) in the firm that my husband's best friend had founded and my son, Henry, had proudly joined.

She said: "You must be in an absolute daze. I told

28

Henry to begin at the beginning and not leave a thing out. We'll have lunch in front of the fire.''

We'd reached the living room, where Henry was fencing with the blaze and Loki lay curled on the sofa. He accepted my tearful embrace without opening his eyes (I had, after all, deserted him). Sadd, glass in hand, sat with shoeless feet extended to the fire.

He said: ''When people ask me how I can stand living in Florida I reply that my feet are never cold there.''

''Hear, hear,'' I said, sinking onto the sofa and pulling Loki onto my lap. I kicked off my own shoes and held my feet gratefully to the fire. Tina poured me a glass of wine and sat down beside me. She said: ''Henry, begin.''

''Right.'' He stored the poker and crossed the room to a desk, returning with a notebook. ''But first, I have to ask Sadd a question: how much of the story May told me about the mausoleum is true?''

''All of it, probably,'' said Sadd. ''Did she say that Jim Cavanaugh is buried there alone because his family anathematized him?''

Henry nodded. ''Something like that. And he's rumored to have used some of the crypts to house the bodies of pals who fell out with him. 'Jim's buddies are in there with him,' people still say.''

Tina said: ''Secret midnight burials!—isn't it wonderful? Of course, the cemetery officials stoutly deny any possibility of—''

''What has all this to do with poor May?'' I asked crossly.

''I think''—Henry gazed into the fire with a look of combined concentration and dreaminess I'd so often seen on his father's face—''that the two things might be connected.''

''What two things?'' Sadd and I spoke together.

"May's overdose and the mausoleum."

We just sat there for a minute. Sadd, who'd been flapping his feet at the fire, held them motionless. Then he said what I was about to:

"I thought you said her problem had to do with her daughter's disappearance."

"That too."

5

"HENRY"—TINA JUMPED UP—"IF YOU DON'T
begin at the beginning, they'll go mad." She started
out of the room. "Hen's school van will be here any
minute—be right back."

"OK. Here goes." Henry laid his notebook open on
his knees and sat hunched over it. His father again. I
was beginning to feel a little numb. Sadd hadn't moved.

"About two weeks ago, we got a phone call from
May inviting us to dinner. We were rather surprised. I
hadn't seen her in years, and Tina had never met her.
How old was she, Mom?"

"Late eighties. May was a dazzling debutante before
I was born. Her first year out, she made what was called
a 'brilliant marriage,' and Ellen was born a year later."

"Never broke stride, though," said Sadd.

"No." Memories were crowding in on me. "She and
Frank loved the social whirl. But afterward . . . it was
different."

Henry nodded. "So I gathered. Dad told me about
this case once. It fascinated him. He always wanted to
reopen it, but it was so close to home he thought it
might bring you grief."

Oh, stop, stop. I closed my eyes and stroked Loki's
back.

Henry went on: "Well, of course we went—to dinner, I mean. Tina said she never felt such vibes of suffering. May was very frail but didn't beat around the bush—she knew we were lawyers, we were 'family,' and she wanted us to reopen Ellen's case.''

"It was never closed," said Sadd, his eyes on the fire.

"So I found out." Henry turned a page of his notebook. "It's still on the files of the Salem, Massachusetts, courthouse.''

"Poor May." I was feeling horribly depressed. "What had come over her?"

"Mom, you'd have felt so sorry for her. She said she knew she couldn't last much longer—did you know she had emphysema?—and she wanted to try once more, as she put it, to 'lay Ellen to rest in her mind.' My first impulse was to dissuade her, and Tina tried to, but May was adamant—and so forlorn and ill and—well, Tina and I were both thinking the same thing: it takes a long time to get something like this rolling, and May could be dead before we'd made much headway. So we told her we'd have to have access to files and records, et cetera, and she said yes, she had a lot and could tell us where to get more—all we needed. Then Tina said that since she knew nothing about the case, would May give us a brief synopsis. I expected something general and rambling, but May started right out—'I'd picked up Ellen's prom gown from the dressmaker that afternoon'— and never stopped for half an hour. We were in the living room having coffee, and the only light was the one over the big portrait of Ellen as a child—you've seen it—pink sash, ringlets, hair ribbon—classic Elsie Dinsmore. Honestly, I expected Vincent Price to walk in any minute.''

Sadd pulled on his shoes and stood up. "I'm going to the bathroom. Tell your mother what May told you—

32

I know the story—and don't say anything about the present situation till I get back. I don't want to miss anything new.''

He went out, shoelaces flapping, looking, I thought, rather more stooped than usual.

I said: "I hope this isn't too upsetting for Sadd. He remembers it all, you see.''

Henry said: "Mom, I feel like a louse.''

"Darling, you had no choice. I wouldn't have wanted you to handle it alone. You did exactly right to bring us. Besides''—I swallowed hard—"you said your dad . . .''

"Always wanted to have a go at this one. Wouldn't he be proud to know that you—''

"You and I. You and I.'' I would *not* be emotional. I put Loki down on the rug and made my voice calm. "Poor, poor May. You said her brother-in-law, Tully, found her this morning?''

"Yes. Thank God he was there to handle it.''

Teresita appeared at this moment bearing sandwiches and coffee and proceeded to set little trays before us. I'd been hungry, but now my mouth was dry, and I knew it would be hard to swallow. Henry spread some loose pages on his tray. While he was talking, Tina came back and stood eating a sandwich and looking at the fire.

"On the night of June 11, 1938, Miss Hammond's School for Girls held its graduation dance as usual at the Eastern Shores Yacht Club in Gloucester, Massachusetts. Miss Hammond's, which folded in 1958, was located in the posh, north-of-Boston town of Wenham but always held this dance at the Eastern Shores because most of the students' parents were members there. The club was very old, very distinguished, and''—Henry peered at his notes—"'restricted.' What does that mean?''

33

I said: "No Jewish members."

Henry snorted. "Well, holy shit, then didn't it just get what it deserved!"

"What did it get?" I was bewildered.

Tina said: "He means all the bad publicity about the Ellen thing."

"Oh, it got much better than that." Henry grinned and waved a clipping. "That charming joint burned to the ground in 1949 with"—he looked at the clipping—" 'heavy financial loss.' Let's hope the loss was 'restricted.' Members only."

Tina, whose mother was Jewish, looked bored. She said: "Get on with it, Henry."

" 'Ellen Dawson, graduating with honors from Miss Hammond's, had celebrated her eighteenth birthday a few weeks before. She was the only child of Frank and May Dawson, who live in Boston and summer in the fashionable'—that word is all over this account—'Bass Rocks section of Gloucester. Their cottage'—another throw-back word—'was next to that of Mrs. Dawson's sister, Irene Hewitt, and her husband, Tully. The brothers-in-law were partners in the brokerage firm of Dawson, Hewitt, and Jerome.' "

Henry turned a page. I put my half-eaten sandwich back on my plate.

"Ellen wanted to go to college and study medicine. We gather that most of her classmates wanted to 'come out' and study marriage. It appears that she was that unique thing, a pretty, brainy girl who was popular with boys and girls alike."

"Sounds like me." said Tina, plopping down on the sofa beside me.

I loved this girl. I said: "But probably not as lucky as you, dear. Your folks were proud as punch when you

34

decided on law school. I'd guess May was more disappointed than proud that Ellen wanted a career.''

Henry nodded. ''I gather that back in her day May was the super-duper deb-of-the-year. She probably hoped that Ellen would follow in her distinguished footsteps. Anyway . . .'' His voice grew somber. ''The end was near.''

Tina's shoulder touching mine was comforting. Henry hunched over his notes, his hands in his hair.

''Ellen's date for the prom was a boy named Foster Warren, who was a senior at Roxbury Latin School in Boston. Ellen was to be taken, not home after the dance, but to her aunt and uncle's, which was virtually the same thing; she had spent all her summers in and out of the big house next door. Uncle Tully and Aunt Irene, who had no children of their own, were like second parents. The reason for the arrangement that night, May explained to us, was that her husband had not been well all week and she didn't want him waked up when Ellen, and possibly some of her friends, checked in around two A.M. Ellen had also dressed next door at Uncle and Aunty's, popped over to show Daddy her prom gown, gave him and Mom a kiss . . . and they never saw her again.''

We sat still for a few seconds, then Tina said:

''That's pretty much all May told us that night. Since then she's sent us tons of material, and we've also done some research on our own. Shall I give Clara a few vital statistics?''

Henry nodded and lay back in his chair, his eyes closed.

Tina started: ''Foster picked Ellen up about nine, and they drove—'' She stopped. Was it something in my face? I felt utterly wretched. She said briskly: ''It can wait. Here's Sadd. Get to yesterday, Henry.''

Henry said: "You talk, hon. You got the phone call."

Tina pondered for a moment, then said: "It was about nine o'clock yesterday morning. I was just leaving to take Hen for a haircut when the phone rang. I called to Teresita to take it and say I'd be home in an hour, but she came out of the kitchen and said I'd better talk to Mrs. Dawson, who was upset. 'Upset' was putting it mildly. May was practically incoherent—and coughing of course—and at first I thought she must be going on about Lloyd because she'd called the day before to talk about that mausoleum business. Finally, it came through: She'd been trying to get Henry at the office because something frightening had happened. She'd just gotten an anonymous letter in the mail telling her to drop the Ellen investigation."

Sadd sat forward in his chair. I couldn't move.

"I said I'd get in touch with Henry—fortunately I knew the client he was with—and I asked May if she'd like me to come over and stay with her. She said, oh, yes, please, that her brother-in-law, Tully, had arrived the night before, down from Boston for Lloyd's funeral, but that he'd gone out to Rye to see some friends and she was alone and the letter had just come and it frightened her. I called Henry, and he said he'd meet me there. I took Hen with me because I wasn't sure how long we'd be, and Teresita goes home at five. We arrived at 740 Park almost together and took the elevator up to May's and walked into her apartment while she was talking to you and Sadd on the phone."

Henry said: "I knew the minute I spoke to you that she hadn't mentioned the letter or Ellen. I think asking you to come for Lloyd's funeral was just a desperate excuse to have more family here to talk to."

I knew it.

Sadd said: "What did the letter say?"

36

"Funny." Henry took a white envelope from his breast pocket. "It's everything an anonymous letter usually isn't. It's not sinister or threatening. It's almost . . . loving."

As he read it, I felt myself dissolving.

Do not, I beg you, pursue the investigation of your daughter's disappearance. You will only open yourself to fresh tragedy. Let her rest—or live—in peace. This is not so much a warning as an urgent and caring request.

"Oh, God, it's from Ellen!" I gasped and burst into tears.

They all spoke and moved at the same time.

Sadd said: "No, Clara, not necessarily," and held out his hand.

Henry said: "Mom, I'm so sorry," and stood up helplessly.

Tina said: "Enough of this. You're going upstairs for a rest," and pulled me to my feet.

I mopped up and apologized for making a scene. Sadd had reached for the letter, and I moved over to look at it with him.

Five lines typed with a faded ribbon.

Sadd said: "It was too much for her. This is why May took the overdose."

"That's what we figured," said Tina.

Sadd looked at me and I guess I nodded, but I was thinking no, no. . . .

I said: "Henry, who else besides you and Tina knew the case was to be reopened?"

"Hard to say." He took the letter from Sadd. "We certainly didn't discuss it with anybody. Of course, May had contacted the courthouse in Salem and the newspapers in the area for back records, et cetera, but as for anyone else she might have told, I can't say."

"I can," said Sadd. "She told me."

6

THE OTHER TWO FACES CONFRONTING SADD
must have worn the same look as mine, because he said
defensively:

"You don't have to look at me like that. I didn't write
the damn thing. What's the postmark, Henry?"

"Radio City Station, day before yesterday, 8 A.M."
said Henry from memory.

"We're not thinking you wrote it." I was beginning
to feel what my son calls "pissed." "We're just thinking you're a rat not to tell us sooner—at least I am!
When did May confide in you?" I knew I was sputter-
ing. "Couldn't you in decency—"

"Time out!" Tina moved determinedly. "Clara,
you're going straight upstairs." She pulled me to the
door as Sadd stood looking properly hangdog and Henry
reached for the bourbon.

I was still blubbering as Tina threw pillows on the
daybed in their little upstairs study and pushed me down
gently. Henry always joked about this "mini guest
room," but I loved it because it was next to Hen's room
and had all their books and games.

"Sadd should have told me." I said for the third or
fourth time.

"Has it occurred to you"—Tina put an afghan over

me—"that ethics might be involved here? Possibly May swore him to secrecy."

"He should have told me anyway." To hell with ethics.

Tina laughed and said she thought she agreed with me, which made me feel better, and I asked what time we had to leave for the—what was it called?

"Wake. Nice old word. To stay awake with the dead. Some people think it's barbaric."

"No more so than cremation before you're cold," I sniveled.

"Nobody's thought of a good way yet." Tina was at the door. "Try to rest. As if you can. But, as my grand-mother used to say, at least you're 'off your feet.' "

She went away closing the door, and I lay there stew-ing, light-years from sleep. Should I try to sort my thoughts or should I say to myself (as I'm told Churchill did on retiring) "the absolute and utter hell with every-thing" and count sheep? Why did I think something had happened to precipitate May's action? Wait—I hadn't decided on thought-sorting yet. Better to count—not sheep—they were boring—but what? The games on the shelf beside me were near enough to read their names without my glasses.

Candyland . . . Chutes and Ladders . . . Monopoly . . . Chinese Checkers—Wouldn't a strong-minded woman like May be, if anything, spurred on by that letter? That letter, the more frightening for its benign-ity? Clara, keep counting.

Tic-tac-toe . . . Uno . . . Backgammon—No, Ellen couldn't have written it. If she's alive, a woman my age now, would she be so pitiless as not to reveal herself unless . . . unless her fate had been so unhallowed . . . Clara, you're in Stephen King country. Keep counting.

Parcheesi . . . Yatzee . . . Connect Four—Henry had

said there might be a connection between Ellen's disappearance and the mausoleum. Surely nothing so macabre as . . . Clara, you're going bonkers. Start again, don't stop, and you may sleep.

Candyland . . . Chutes and Ladders . . . Monopoly—

The door opened a foot, and Henry put his head in. "You OK, Mom?"

"Of course, dear. Sit here." I patted the bed beside me and he sat down, his head silhouetted against the frost on the window. Oh, beloved, familiar silhouette, even to the cowlick standing spikily up.

"Mom, I'll never forgive myself if you get too psyched—"

"All I am is a little tired. An hour's rest here and I'll be fine."

"Tina and I have been talking. We don't think you should go to the wake tonight."

"Certainly I'm going. End of discussion."

Henry smiled. "Well, not tomorrow for May. The rest of us will go up to White Plains if you'll stay here with Hen. It's Teresita's day off."

"That's a deal." I sat up on one elbow. "And I'll promise not to get 'psyched' if you'll tell me this: Why do you think there's a connection between May's death and the mausoleum?"

Henry sat still for a minute, then he said: "It's far-fetched, but I think it has to be considered. The summer before Ellen disappeared she worked for Jim Cavanaugh for a while—as a lark—May kept stressing 'as a lark' and I gather she hadn't approved. Suppose Jim had made a play for Ellen, and she hadn't bought it and—well, he was a vengeful guy, and there are all those stories about how he stashed bodies in the crypts.

41

I don't know if such a thought ever occurred to May, but it did to me when I saw that anonymous letter.''

Henry stopped talking, and I lay back feeling 'psyched' and trying not to show it. "It's pretty awful."

"Yes. Sadd says it's grotesque. He won't even discuss it.''

There were a lot of things Sadd wouldn't discuss, I thought impatiently, but this was not the moment to talk about May's death.

I said: "What became of the boy who took Ellen to the prom?''

"Foster Warren? He was killed at Anzio four years later.''

"I suppose he was thoroughly—what do you call it—?''

"Questioned. Interrogated. Grilled. In spades. So were the other two kids.''

"Other two?''

"It was a foursome that night. Foster and Ellen drove to Marblehead to pick up a friend of Ellen's and her date. They were all four seen at the prom and then— according to the other three, and they never deviated from their story—they went for a swim off Bass Rocks just down the road from the Dawson house: that is, the boys did, and Ellen ran home to get swimsuits for herself and the other girl. They never saw her again.''

I lay there trying to take this in. "She never went into her house for the swimsuits?''

"Wasn't seen if she did.''

"And she never showed up at Irene and Tully's?''

Henry shook his head. "They waited up till all hours. By the way, Tully's downstairs. He's going with us to-night.''

"Who was the other girl?''

42

"Her name was Susan Lozier. She married an Englishman and died last year."

"And the other boy?"

"You may meet him tonight." Henry stood up. "Peter Angier, an old friend of Sadd's. He married one of the Cavanaugh girls and she died and he's remarried—I don't know who to. A fine rest you're having. Stay put. We'll eat about six. Just pizza."

He kissed me and went out. I stared at the door for a minute, then went determinedly back to my count.

Checkers . . . Chess . . . Tiddly Winks . . . Cribbage—

The door, which had remained ajar, was pushed open, and Tina appeared with a steaming mug.

"Henry said you were awake. This is Ovaltine—don't laugh—my mother still drinks it."

"Who's laughing?" I accepted the mug and turned on my side. "So Tully's here."

"Yes. Sadd's got him in front of the fire. Rather a forlorn creature, isn't he? I'd never met him."

Tina went to the window to watch for Hen's van, and I sipped my Ovaltine while trying to recall Tully Hewitt's face . . . long, pleasant, horsey, not handsome. He was younger than his wife, Irene, I remembered, and still lived in the house that had figured in the tragedy, Sadd had said—at which instant, that reprobate appeared in the door.

"Go away, I'm not speaking to you," I said and held my empty mug out to Tina. "Thank you, dear."

"Here's the van." Tina waved to someone in the street and went out.

Sadd said: "Clara, you're being childish."

"So leave. You're not overly fond of children."

"Now, listen to me." He planted his feet in the aggravated troll stance. "When I got a letter from May

43

ten days ago, how was I to know she was going to die? She asked me not to say anything to you yet. She assumed you'd gone to Florida to 'rest and forget this sort of thing,' which you had and which I thought rather sensitive of May to consider. I immediately wrote back begging her not to do this—the very thought appalled me—and how could I know she'd already engaged Henry, gotten the ball rolling, and left herself open to that letter? I've just explained this to Henry and Tina, and they admitted they themselves were hesitant to involve you. So everyone who cares about you was trying to spare you, and you should be grateful."

Grudgingly, I said I supposed I was. Then I said: "How's Tully taking this?"

"Badly. You won't know him. He's not much older than I am and he looks a hundred. I have the impression he's been boozing for years and shocks like this don't help."

"Did he know of May's plan to reopen the case?"

"Not till yesterday. He was in Rye all day visiting friends, and when he called May to say he'd be back in time to take her to dinner, Henry answered the phone and had to tell him why he was there and about the letter, et cetera. Tully took the first train he could back to Grand Central." Sadd peered at the bookshelf over my head.

"Anything decent to read here?"

I tried to make my voice casual. "Did Henry and Tina wait at May's till Tully arrived?"

"No, as a matter of fact—" Sadd stopped, eyeing me. "You're not going to start that again."

"I asked you a question."

He heaved a sigh. "No, May urged them to leave. She said she felt better, and since she knew Tully would be back soon, which he was, there was no reason for

44

them to stay. Hen was getting restless, so they took off. When Tully got back—he just told me this—he took May out to dinner and had a long imploring talk with her of the kind I had planned—"

"So May was alone for better than an hour."

"By golly, so she was!" When Sadd gets sarcastic, he tends to overdo it. "Completely alone and unprotected! And whoever came in during that convenient hour and forced her own prescription stuff down her throat—"

"Oh, for heaven's sake let me get some rest." I turned over and closed my eyes. "And you'd better do the same or you know what's going to happen; you're going to fall asleep at that wake tonight."

"I sincerely hope so," said Sadd and went off.

Scrabble . . . Mah-Jongg . . . Pinochle . . .

So many ways to kill people. You can wait and watch, then appear suddenly from across the years or across the street, and you can bully or blackmail or threaten or lament, and you can leave, as guilty of someone's self-destruction as if you had slain her where she stood. It would be murder, murder that *worked*, just as Ellen's murder, if there had been one, had worked for fifty years . . . fifty years . . . fifty years . . .

I realized dimly, joyfully, that I was falling asleep. Could it really be possible?—that lovely lifting, swimming, floating. . . . Was I actually to have a priceless interlude of nothingness? Even my feet, cold since my arrival, were warm. . . . Maybe I'm dying, I thought lazily. But *warm feet*? This was heaven in advance. I moved them and the warmth shifted and meowed. Loki! Oh, darling cat, you found me! I'd reach down and stroke you but I'm gone . . . I'm really gone. . . .

The door opened.

"Gran, why do monkeys wear green suspenders to bed?"

7

I LOVED THE KITCHEN OF THIS HOUSE, AN OB-
long room in the center of which Tina had put an old
refectory table and wooden chairs. She and Henry had
"modernized" (a word Sadd refuses to use) only to the
extent of the appliances; big windows and old-fashioned
cabinets remained. The pantry housed a small black-
and-white television to which Hen was allowed to re-
pair, providing the volume was kept down to candle
power.

He sat there now on a stool, and beside him sat Loki,
who made an occasional decrepit pass at Hen's pizza
and was rewarded with tendrils of cheese. The rest of
us sat at the table munching our own delectable slices,
conscious that Tully's presence made us less comfortable than we'd been with just each other. He talked
incessantly, devouring the pizza, his thin legs crossed
and sliding around on the wooden seat of his chair.

"Thank heaven I'm out of May's apartment. I'd have
gone batty before long what with the police and the
coroner and calls from other people in the place."

Henry said: "You saved us all that, Tully."

"Glad I could. Your wife's call was the only nice
one. You certainly married a mighty kind little lady,
Henry." Managing to sound both courtly and corny,
Tully beamed at Tina.

So he hadn't just shown up: Tina had invited him. Typical.

She said quickly: "I'm glad you could get a cab in this weather."

"It wasn't too bad in Manhattan. You caught it worse here. Is there any more of that great coffee? Actually, I love the snow. I guess I'm just a confirmed old Yankee. I brought an extra vest for you, Sadd. A wool one."

"Thank you. It should fit fine," said Sadd. "Not more than twenty pounds difference between us. I'll wear it with Henry Gamadge's overcoat and be the fashion plate of the wake tonight."

"Speaking of tonight"—Henry was pouring coffee all around—"let me make a little speech: We five are in a rather unique position—"

"You don't qualify 'unique,' " said Sadd. "You can't be 'rather' unique or 'very' unique—"

"Oh, be quiet, Sadd," I said. "Go on, Henry."

"In deference to our grammarian"—Henry returned the coffee pot to the stove—"let me put it this way: We five know of May's pitiful plan to reopen Ellen's case. It would be comforting to think that we alone know of it, but since all of us have disclaimed sending that anonymous letter, we must assume that someone else with access to a New York City postbox within the last week also knows. That someone could be the shadowy Ellen herself, or someone who learned of the matter through the sources May contacted."

"Or," said Tully, "someone else she told."

"Exactly." Henry stirred his coffee. "In fact, someone who could be at the wake tonight."

We sat in silence for a few seconds, then he added: "So naturally, we should say nothing about the matter to anyone."

Then Tina said what we'd all agreed to say for Tully's sake: "Anyway, it ends with May's death."

Tully drew a shaky breath. "I don't think I'd have survived it. I really don't."

"She dreaded telling you, Tully," Henry said gently. "She knew it would bring back all the old pain."

Tully stood up. "Do you mind if I put a drop of brandy in my coffee? I brought some."

We all became very busy clearing the table as Tully went to his coat on a rack near the kitchen door.

Sadd said: "Has it occurred to any of you that we will also probably be the only ones at the wake who know that May is dead?"

We stopped carrying and looked at each other. Henry said slowly: "She died early this morning. . . . Tina called the obituary in for tomorrow's papers. . . . You're right, Sadd."

I said: "Maybe we shouldn't mention that either."

"I agree." Tina was rinsing plates. "If only for the poor widow's sake. One death at a time."

"Won't she be missed?" asked Henry.

"May's been 'missed' for fifty years." Sadd said it almost absently, but the effect on us was instant and somber. I broke the silence.

"I wonder if anybody other than family who learns of May's death will remember about Ellen."

Tully said, sipping his spiked coffee: "Crimes of that type are pretty much forgotten in fifty years—unless your name happens to be Lindbergh."

"This wasn't a crime," said Sadd, "it was a disappearance. It isn't a crime to disappear."

"You know what I mean."

Indeed we did. Heartbreak and ruined lives are not crimes; they are much, much worse. Tully went on, the brandy already making him lugubrious:

48

"We were all so close, so close. My wife was May's sister. That's why we built next door to them in Gloucester."

Sadd and I looked at each other, and I could swear he was thinking what I was thinking. Why this recitation of known facts? Why is it the essence of a bore—granted, a tortured one—to prolong the account with which he has the floor by piling on givens?

"Frank Dawson and I were partners in Dawson, Hewitt, and Jerome. Irene and I never had any children. We adored Ellen. She was only my niece by marriage but I was just as fond—"

He stopped short, gulped his coffee, and began again:

"Do you know that last night May and I talked about Ellen for the first time in years? We went out to dinner—I took her to La Maison Bleue on Eighty-sixth Street—and I was able to say 'May, dear, don't do it, don't start this terrible business, for *her* sake don't.' She was quite calm—I don't know if I'd persuaded her—and when we got home she went to bed almost at once."

Sadd said: "Tully, when did you last see May alive?"

More gulping. "The police asked me that and I didn't know how to answer. After she went to bed, I watched TV for an hour or so and then—in case she was still awake—I opened her door a little bit and said 'Good night, May, dear,' and she didn't move, and I went to bed. This morning when I knocked on her door and she didn't answer—well, Henry knows what I told him when I phoned him—but how could I tell the police"—his voice began to go—"I could very well be responsible for May's death because she might have been so upset by our talk—"

"Tully, dear." I put my hand on his arm. "It's over.

49

Let's have no talk of responsibility. Now, I want to know your plans. How long will you be here?''

"Well, it depends." Tully blew his nose. "There's Lloyd's funeral and May's committal both tomorrow. How do we decide who goes to which?"

Sadd said: "If I go to Lloyd's wake tonight I've done him full justice. Those R.C. funeral Masses can be interminable. All that singing."

Tina said: "The singing at Lloyd's should be worth it. It'll be his own choir, and they say it's magnificent."

Sadd grunted, and Henry said: "I'd say our first duty is to May. We'll probably be the only ones there. Mother has offered to stay home with Hen, so the four of us will go to White Plains tomorrow. Tonight it'll be another foursome. Tina's not going to the wake."

I was briefly surprised, then understood when Tina said her sitter's mother didn't allow weeknights. "So you'd all better get a move on. Come on, Hen, bedtime."

Hen stalled with all the classic requests for more dessert, something to drink, a story, then repeated hugs all around and was finally marched off. I took Loki in my arms and sat down again at the kitchen table, overwhelmed with reluctance to budge. The other three proposed mourners went into the pantry to get the weather channel and returned with the depressing word that the forecast was excellent—clear skies, well-plowed streets, and other regrettably good conditions.

Sadd said grimly: "Onward, Christian soldiers," and we went for our coats.

By the time we reached the Long Island Expressway, my feet had turned to ice. (Sadd's boast that in Florida one's feet are never cold was not an idle one.) I thrust them under the heater vent, and Henry pulled off his scarf and told me to wrap them in it. Another scarf, borrowed from Tully, was wrapped around my head, making my hair a mare's nest. The wool suit, which I'd left with Tina after the Christmas visit, itched because I'd forgotten to bring a blouse, and the one she'd loaned me was too tight and admitted tortuous, tweedy hairs at every seam.

In the back seat, Sadd was being fiercely argumentative about Florida, Tully having stated that it was the last place he'd ever want to visit, let alone live. Henry, bless him, said some nice things about Santa Martina Island (he and Tina had visited us), but Tully was the complete Philistine; he'd heard that Florida was a wasteland of tackiness.

"Some of it is, Tully," I said over my shoulder. Then, heaping coals of fire, a Biblical injunction I've always considered strange in phrasing but saintly in practice, I added: "Anyway, why would you ever want to leave Gloucester and that lovely house at Bass Rocks?"

Sadd said, using the defensive Floridian's last-ditch weapon: "Aren't your heating bills pretty bad?"

"Not really. I don't live in the whole house anymore. When Irene died, I closed off the second floor and made the dining room into my bedroom."

My turn. "I remember that wonderful breeze from the Atlantic that filled every room. . . ."

"I insulated ten years ago. Snug as a bug now."

The heck with it. I gave up and reflected with genuine pleasure on the image of the handsome old frame house with its widow's walk and the wide veranda overlooking the beautiful and treacherous rocks of Gloucester's coast.

The white line on the expressway crawled by on my right.

Henry said: "I don't dare go any faster."

"Please don't," I said. "Where's the funeral home?"

"Queens Village. Not far from the expressway, thank heaven. I have the exit number here in my pocket." He fished for it and then said: "Tully, before we get there— since we're all sworn to silence on the Ellen matter— I'd like to ask you a question, if it won't be too painful for you to talk about it."

Tully said no, of course not, and in the darkness of the car, question and answer seemed to flash before us like lantern slides of a long-ago summer.

"I'm curious about an episode I dug up in Ellen's rather overprotected life. It seems she worked for Jim Cavanaugh one summer. Do you remember that?"

"Vividly. It was the summer before she graduated. The job came about as an afterthought to a visit with the Martin Cavanaughs in Patchogue, Long Island."

"She hadn't gone expressly to work for Jim?"

"Good God, no. Her parents would never have let her."

"How did the job happen?"

Tully sighed. "Martin and Sara had a big family, as you know, and their eldest daughter was Ellen's age. The girls hadn't seen each other in some years. May was always rather snobby toward her sister's family— Irish Catholic and all that. I thought they were charming. Anyway, Sara invited Ellen down for a visit—their summer place in Patchogue was very nice—Martin did all right—and Frank told me they were going to let Ellen go. Perhaps they felt it was about time Ellen saw someplace besides the north shore of Boston. In any event, she went."

I'd forgotten my cold feet and was hoping we wouldn't arrive before Tully finished.

"As I got the story from Frank afterwards—May was

52

so angry, she never spoke of it—what impressed Ellen most was that her Cavanaugh cousins—those around her age—all had summer jobs. They worked in shops and restaurants around Patchogue and apparently had fun. Ellen thought this was great—she was that kind of girl— and maybe she felt a bit useless hanging around with the younger kids all day. Then one morning, Jim Cavanaugh showed up.'' Tully cleared his throat. "Now, remember, I got all this second hand, some from Frank, some from Ellen—"

"We remember," I said.

"Well, Jim was still something of a pariah because of the bootlegging years—did you know that his own wife died from the stuff?—but now he'd started a legitimate contracting business and was trying to get in the family's good graces. He'd come to invite Martin's brood out to his splashy new beach house in Far Rockaway, but at the moment he arrived Sara was out, the kids were on the beach, and Ellen was the only one home. He'd never seen her before."

In the silence that followed, I thought: And her name was Dawson. A name he hated.

The car slowed, and Henry said: "Here's our exit. Everybody keep an eye out for the Mowry Brothers Funeral Home about a mile up on the left. Talk fast, Tully. Jim offered Ellen a job?"

"Not only offered but said he'd pick her up every morning and deliver her home at night. His office was twenty minutes away, and she could do some filing, answer the phone, et cetera. The fact that she'd never been inside an office except when she went into Boston to have lunch with her father—what matter? And Ellen, of course, was delighted. Cousin Jim was 'an old sweetie.' I remember her exact expression, 'an old sweetie.' "

Sadd said dryly: "Jim would have been thrilled. Let's see—he'd have been late forties, maybe fifty. What did he look like, Tully?"

"I never saw him."

I said: "How did Ellen ever square this with her parents?"

"They were in Europe. They decided to go when Ellen went to Patchogue, and they weren't expected back for six weeks. I gather Martin and Sara did have some qualms about allowing the job, but maybe they felt it would do Ellen good to get some practical experience. Of course, when Frank and May came back, all hell broke loose. Ellen was pulled home overnight, and May never spoke to her sister again."

We rode for a while, subdued by the depressing conclusion of the story. Then Henry said:

"How much longer after that did Jim die?"

"A couple of years." Tully's voice was weary. "He had an 'accidental' fall from one of his buildings. It was an open secret he'd been fighting with some of his former associates, and one of them probably shoved him. Anyway, he was buried in that awful place he'd built, disgraced to the end. And then came those preposterous rumors about his having buried other bodies there, which is such hogwash because that cemetery is very secured—even families don't have keys to the mausoleums—you have to get one at the office when there's a burial—"

"Here we are," said Henry. Arc lights blazed up on our left, flooding a packed parking lot. "Will you look at the cars!"

I started to unwrap my feet and said: "I wonder if anybody ever asked Ellen point-blank if Jim made a pass at her."

Tully said primly: "I certainly never asked her."

"Of course"—Henry turned into the lot—"she probably would have kept it to herself if he had—might even have liked it."

Tully suddenly went from prim to passionate. "You'd never say that if you knew Ellen Dawson! She was the sweetest, most honorable—"

"Oh, come on, Tully"—Henry expressed my own irritation—"she was a woman."

"She was *seventeen*!" Tully's voice shook. "And before we close the subject, I'd like to say that I entirely concurred with her parents' actions, even to returning Jim's insulting Christmas present."

Henry had squeezed the Datsun into a compact space, and we were piling out stiffly. We stopped, in various stages of emergence, looking at Tully.

"What was it?" I said.

"He sent her a diamond wristwatch which must have been worth a thousand dollars."

We started walking toward the welcoming glow of the canopy. A thousand dollars in 1938. . . . Well, I thought, with a spasm of amusement, there are insults and there are insults.

Henry said: "Did Ellen know about the insulting Christmas present?"

"I don't know." Tully began to walk ahead of us. "I only saw her in the summers, and the next summer she was gone."

THE MOWRY BROTHERS FUNERAL HOME, AP-
parently a former spacious private residence, was
jammed.

8

THE MOWRY BROTHERS FUNERAL HOME, AP-
parently a former spacious private residence, was
jammed.

As we inserted ourselves into the crowd, which extended even to the front door, a sign was being hoisted:
MORE SEATING UPSTAIRS. The recitation of the rosary
was in progress (a ritual that I have always considered
beautiful), and voices rose and fell around us.

Sadd whispered: "We infidels are going upstairs,"
and he and Henry disappeared. I looked at Tully, but
he was standing patiently beside me, apparently resigned to waiting out the devotions. Well, I myself didn't
mind standing for a while after the cramped discomfort
of the car, and my feet were warming up nicely. I un-
wrapped the scarf from my head and a low voice beside
me said: "Can't miss that handsome heap of hair.
Hello, Aunt Clara."

It was Jonathan Saddlier, Sadd's son.

"Jon, dear! I'm so glad to see you!" I'd always liked
this boy. Good-looking, early thirties, single, Jon made
an adequate living with a music publisher and dreamed
of becoming an opera star. His voice, according to
Sadd, was "not good enough and not bad enough" to
settle his fate, so he continued with the singing lessons

he couldn't afford and, as I would platitudinize to his father, "after all, it's his life."

I said: "My 'handsome heap' must look a mess." I touched my hair self-consciously, wondering why I couldn't take an offhand compliment more gracefully.

"Not a bit—you could go on as the empress in *L'Aiglon*. I was hoping you and Dad might come north for this. Is he here?"

"Yes, upstairs. Do you remember your cousin Tully?"

Tully nodded at Jon, then put his finger to his lips. A few heads had turned disapprovingly. Jon took my arm, whispered "Let's go aloft," and piloted me to the stairs.

I said: "I didn't realize you knew Lloyd."

"I didn't, until last year. My voice coach told me to go listen to his choir at St. Bernard's. When I introduced myself, the Saddlier-Cavanaugh connection came up. Lloyd was a great choral director. Wait till you hear his High Requiem tomorrow."

I was spared having to say that I would not hear it by our arrival at MORE SEATING UPSTAIRS and by Sadd's delight at seeing Jon. He adored his son, despite the fall of genes that had made them so different. Henry was filling coffee cups from an urn that stood at one end of the room. A dozen or more persons had found their way here, and one of them, a hunched figure in a chair near the urn, looked as if he had found his way from a soup kitchen. He was clutching a coffee cup and staring into space, a shriveled man who could have been sixty or ninety, encased in a deplorable overcoat buttoned to the neck.

Jon said, as we sat down on the folding chairs being placed for us: "There's poor old Marty Cavanaugh. I should go speak to him, but he's so skittish."

57

"Marty?" Sadd looked across the room with interest. "Son of Martin and Sara?"

"I don't know whose son he is, Dad. He's just your old-fashioned family drunk. Lloyd was good to him. Marty used to go over to St. Bernard's sometimes on Sunday morning to get out of the cold and listen to the music. Lloyd would always take him out to breakfast. Did you know that St. Bernard's is up for some kind of papal award because of Lloyd? It's one of the few Catholic churches in New York that still keeps the authentic Gregorian chant with full choir."

"That's interesting," I said, my eyes on the hunched figure across the room.

"And refreshing," said Jon. "All you get in most churches today is the congregation bleating in the pews."

"Who's bleeding in the pews?" asked Sadd. I knew his attention had wandered to where mine had.

"Bleating, Dad. Singing off-key and not knowing all the lyrics."

I said the "lyrics" of hymns had always been my downfall as Henry approached, balancing three cups of coffee. He distributed them, shook hands with Jon, and said, as he sat down:

"That sad-looking creature over there is Martin Cavanaugh, Junior. I introduced myself and when he told me his name, I said 'you must be Jim Cavanaugh's nephew' and he said yes and kept drinking his coffee—which is spiked to the hilt, by the way."

Jon waved to someone across the room and excused himself. Sadd and Henry and I looked at each other. Tully's recounting of the events of that summer was still perking.

Sadd said: "Martin would be one of those cousins in Patchogue. He'd have known Ellen."

"And Jim," said Henry. "Wouldn't you love to pump him on the subject of the mausoleum?"

I said: "We shouldn't all converge on him. Jon described him as 'skittish.'"

"I'd describe him as drunk," said Henry.

"Jon also said Lloyd was good to him." Then I added: "I wonder if Lloyd remembered Jim Cavanaugh."

"Too bad we can't ask him." Sadd drained his coffee. "But I doubt it. Lloyd's father was a much older brother of Jim's. He took off for Ohio during Prohibition while Jim was distinguishing himself in New York. Lloyd was born and raised out there."

Across the room, the bedraggled figure of Martin Cavanaugh stood up and I thought nervously—we're going to lose him. . . . Sadd and Henry straightened too. But Martin had only turned to the coffee urn and was now, without the least attempt to be covert, doctoring his cup.

A voice behind us said: "It's Sadd Saddlier—it has to be!"

Sadd turned and said: "It's Peter Angier—it has to be!"

Henry and I were introduced to a very tall, nice-looking man with thinning white hair and a crisp mustache. As he and Sadd chatted away, I whispered to Henry: "Ellen's friend's date?" and he nodded. I sighed, wishing I could say: "Do come and sit by me and tell me all about that terrible night fifty years ago when Ellen Dawson disappeared and did you by any chance recently write an anonymous letter—" Sadd was saying:

"Pete and I went to our first dance together at Miss Long's School on Fifty-fourth Street, and my date fell madly in love with him. I tried to drop his acquaintance after that but was never able to manage it.''

''He nearly managed it when he went to Florida''— Peter Angier was smiling at me—''but my wife and I are moving to Sarasota next winter. I hope you'll be visiting again, Mrs. Gamadge.''

I murmured something as Jon returned with word that prayers were over and he thought we'd better go down and pay our respects. With one accord, three pairs of eyes turned longingly in the direction of Martin Cavanaugh. I said:

''Please go ahead—I'll follow you in a minute. I'm going to the ladies' room,'' and headed for a sign which was, happily, in the general direction of Martin. The room was filling up fast, but he sat, still quite alone, staring before him. I refilled my cup from the coffee urn and sat down next to him.

I said: ''What a lot of people. Lloyd Cavanaugh must have been much admired. I didn't know him well, did you?''

Martin didn't turn, but he said slowly: ''He was the nicest person I ever knew.''

''I keep hearing that. My name is Clara Gamadge, by the way. May I ask yours?''

Still slowly, still without turning: ''Martin Cavanaugh.''

''Oh, a relation of Lloyd's? I'm not actually *related* to the family—just sort of, well, *connected*, you might say''—my, how chatty I was—''and I do remember some of the older Cavanaughs. Let's see . . . are you any relation to Jim Cavanaugh?''

Now Martin turned and looked at me groggily: ''You're the second person who's asked me that tonight. I thought we didn't mention good old Uncle Jim in this family.''

"Really? I understand he was quite colorful. Years ago a cousin of mine, Ellen Dawson, worked for Jim one summer. She liked him."

Martin's eyes came into focus for a minute as he gazed directly into mine. "Did you know Ellen?" I nodded. "Did she . . ." He gave up and his eyes splayed again. "Did she die?"

"You've got me there." I felt like a rat. "I just don't keep up with the family as I should. Tell me more about Lloyd. I suppose he'll be buried in the Dawson Mausoleum in Holy Martyrs."

Ah—my first rise out of Martin. He sat up quite straight and said clearly: "Oh, no. Nobody will ever be buried there except Uncle Jim and his buddies. And me."

I cast a silent prayer up to my husband's spirit to help keep my voice calm. I said: "Now, that's odd. The one thing I remember hearing about that mausoleum is that Jim Cavanaugh is buried there alone."

Martin shook his head. "That's what people think, but I know different."

Another prayer. I wrinkled my brow. "You're probably thinking of Jim's mother. True, she was buried there once, but I believe her body was transferred. Other than that, the place hasn't been opened since Jim died."

"I open it. I open it all the time."

Martin clawed at his neck and got his fingers around a piece of filthy string. A key dangled from it. I thought I knew how Lord Carnarvon felt at the door of King Tut's tomb. I wanted to run yelping to Henry and Sadd. Martin was still talking as he tucked the key back carefully.

"That's where I'm going to be buried, you see. Father Dever took me to the doctor just the other day and you know what he said? He said I'd probably be a holy

61

martyr myself real soon, and they'll lay me away with Uncle Jim and his buddies. Of course''—Martin grew tearful—''I won't have the lovely Mass that Lloyd promised me. He always said he'd bring me over to St. Bernard's and give me the whole works—choir and all. Now he's gone.''

Martin pulled a gruesome handkerchief from his overcoat pocket and wiped his eyes. He added: ''I'd better go home.''

Dear God, we mustn't lose this treasure. ''Perhaps we could give you a ride,'' I said. ''Where do you—I mean—how did you come?''

''Father Dever brought me.'' Martin stood up, listing. ''He said as soon as he finished saying the rosary he'd—''

''Martin,'' I said, ''do sit down again for a minute.'' I gave his arm a mere touch which, in Martin's condition, must have been the equivalent of a push, for down he plopped. ''I have some friends who would love to meet you. Let me find them—and I'll find Father Dever for you, too.''

I threaded my way back to the stairs and went down them on something of a run. From the slight elevation of the bottom step, I gazed around the crowd. Sadd and Henry were nowhere to be seen, and there were Father Devers everywhere. Then I sighted Sadd talking to Helen Cavanaugh beside her husband's coffin. Barbaric to interrupt there; better go back and check on my treasure. I hurried up the stairs again and over to the corner—Martin was gone. Oh, damn, damn. Back to the stairs and down them (I'm certain there were people who returned from the wake to describe an old woman who spent the evening running up and down the stairs) and met Henry midway.

"Henry," I said in his ear, "Martin has a key to the mausoleum—but I've lost him."

"I just saw him"—Henry looked over his shoulder—"going out the door with a priest. A *key*?" Henry had caught the fever. "Let me see if I can find them." He took off.

I made my way over to Sadd and Helen Cavanaugh, and she held out her arms to me.

"Clara, dear, you were wonderful to come."

I embraced her, a tiny woman and a darling person. "Helen, we're all so sorry—and so proud. Lloyd was a great person. I hear nothing but his praises on all sides."

Sadd said: "I always thought that Lloyd fit Cardinal Newman's definition of a gentleman: One who never knowingly inflicts pain."

"Oh, Sadd, how well you knew him!" Helen, who was no dope, knew that Sadd scarcely knew him, but was herself one who never knowingly inflicted pain. "Lloyd would be so honored to think you came tonight. Now I want to hear about Florida."

I suppose we chatted on the subject, but my mind was on Henry searching for Martin-of-the-Key. Now Henry was coming toward us, shaking his head. My heart sank. I said:

"Helen—that nice priest who led the rosary—who was he? Sadd was so impressed with his voice."

Sadd looked nonplussed.

"Oh, Father Dever," said Helen. "He's our pastor at Saint Agnes's in Hollis. Yes, a wonderful speaker. Henry Gamadge, you are the image of you father! And now you'd better take these dear folks home—it may snow again. Say good night to Tully for me. By the way, I think he looks bad."

As we headed for the door, Henry said: "Not only

looks bad but feels worse. I had to take him out to the car.''

"Is he ill?" I was truly concerned.

"Either that or he needed a nip. And I couldn't find Martin, damn it."

"Couldn't find him?" Sadd was puzzled.

"Never mind," I said. "Father Dever saves all."

"And would you mind telling me"—Sadd held the door as we emerged into the piercing cold night air—"why I'm supposed to be impressed with that reverend gentleman's voice—which I have never heard?"

"Because," I said smugly, "it is he who escorts Martin Cavanaugh to wakes and must therefore know where he lives. And Martin is the Cavanaugh who speaks freely of Uncle Jim and his 'buddies' who are buried with him in the mausoleum."

Henry and Sadd stopped walking. Henry said: "You didn't tell me he said that! And he has a key to the place, Sadd."

"A key!"

"A key," I said, pushing them on toward the car, "which he wears like an amulet around his neck."

"Around his neck?"

"My God, it sounds like a fetish!"

We'd arrived at the car, I, a little tipsy with success, to find Tully a little tipsy with brandy and, as we jabbered excitedly, inclined to be a wet blanket.

9

"I THINK YOU'RE ALL BEING GHOULISH. Haven't we been through enough? I certainly have."

We lapsed into rather crestfallen silence as Henry renegotiated the Long Island Expressway and Tully scolded on.

"Why on earth would you even want to go *near* that godawful mausoleum? It's been nothing but a source of humiliation all these—"

"Tully"—Sadd spoke with admirable mildness—"when May called us in Florida yesterday morning [was it really only yesterday morning? I marvelled], she said that if we could just get Lloyd buried in the mausoleum, then we'd all show up for the funeral and the place would be opened—"

"A funeral is different. A funeral's official."

"We weren't contemplating a midnight raid," said Henry.

"You're contemplating going in there unauthorized with some nutty dypso—"

"Tully, the place belongs to us—it's family property." I was trying to keep my temper because, in addition to his churlishness, he had the front seat and the lion's share of the heater. "What we hope to do is to go quietly into the place with Martin's key, and if there's

65

no sign of disturbance, and if it appears that Martin was just drunk and wandering in the head—''

"Which he was," said Tully, hiccoughing.

''—then we'll decide whether to forget the whole thing or whether to ask for an official examination of the crypts. Here's a chance to lay a family skeleton to rest—''

"There is no family skeleton!" Tully was close to shouting. "That vault is empty except for the body of James Cavanaugh. There isn't the remotest chance that anybody could have ever entered that place and taken the stone slab from any of those crypts without the help of cemetery workmen. You don't need a key to see that. You can just stand at the grille and look in."

I was suddenly surprised. "Have you seen the place?"

"Certainly. I went to Jim Cavanaugh's funeral."

The car swerved a little, and I knew how Henry felt. Beside me, Sadd's sharp intake of breath indicated a similar jolt.

"Fascinating," he said in an awed tone. "I was abroad at the time. Whatever made you go?"

"We went as a favor to Sara." Tully was sobering up into sniffles. "She wrote to Irene and me—I told you May wasn't speaking to her—and asked us if we'd come and help make some kind of family showing, so we did. It wasn't pleasant standing there with a handful of relatives and a bunch of reporters in front of that ugly, vulgar pile of marble. Believe me, I never want to see that place again."

Had Tully stood before the mausoleum that day with macabre thoughts? Was he now reliving the sight of the crypts, one, perhaps, with frightful contents? We had all avoided mentioning Ellen's fate and had fastened almost jovially on Jim's "buddies." I began to feel compassion, and Henry's thoughts may have been the same, for he said gently:

"I wish you'd stay with us tonight, Tully."

"Thank you, Henry, but no. May's apartment shouldn't be empty for too long. The papers will be out in a few hours, and people will be calling. And I want to change my clothes."

Sadd said: "Henry, drop your mother off at home and you and I will take Tully—"

"Now, that's *really* out of the question," Tully was scolding again, but kindly. "When you get home, you're going to stay put. A cab brought me over and a cab can take me back. It isn't that late."

Bless you for that, Tully, I thought. We were nearing Brooklyn Heights, and I was suddenly exhausted. None of us spoke for a while. Sadd hummed, a sure sign that his mind was teeming. As we turned into Willow Street, Tully said, with infinite weariness:

"But I would appreciate a ride to White Plains tomorrow. After the service I'll get a cab to LaGuardia."

"Pick you up at nine," said Henry.

The next morning I felt my age.

All night I'd been playing Candyland with a faceless Jim Cavanaugh on Bass Rocks Beach and was barely able to raise my head when Tina looked in and said they were leaving shortly and Hen was watching cartoons.

"Good Lord, Tina, what time is it?"

"About eight. Jon Saddlier's here. He saw the papers and wants to go with us. And Helen Cavanaugh called. She was shocked but thanked us for not springing it last night. Here's the obit."

I felt blindly for my robe. "Read it to me. God knows where my glasses are."

Tina read:

Suddenly at her home in New York City, Jan. 20,
May Saddlier Dawson, widow of Frank W. Dawson,
founder of Dawson, Hewitt, and Jerome. Services
private.

"I tried to make it as noncommital as possible. I
suppose the suicide bit will leak out eventually." Tina
looked at her watch. "Come on down and I'll give you
Hen's schedule."

I pulled on an ancient wool bathrobe of Henry Gamadge's and with my hair still in the braid I make of it
at night, got myself down to the kitchen where Sadd
and Jon stood sipping coffee. Jon kissed me and said:

"Dad says Aunt May took a powder. I feel terrible.
I'm glad I looked at the paper this morning. I wish
you'd all told me last night."

Sadd said: "We didn't think you'd want to miss
Lloyd's funeral and all that glorious chanting."

"I hope to be back for most of it. The Mass doesn't
start till eleven. Did you know I'd been in touch with
May recently, and she put some money in that opera?"

We all looked at him in some surprise. Jon added:
"Even when it failed, she was nice and said to ask her
again. By the way, what becomes of her money?"

Now we looked at each other. It had not occurred—
to me, at least—to ask.

Tina said: "Henry knows her lawyer. He'll call him
today. Clara, Hen's lunch . . ." She went on to say
something about grilled cheese, but my mind had
snagged on the thought of May's will. She'd been a
wealthy woman with no immediate family. How had the
long, sad years affected her thinking, her decisions?
"—and chocolate milk," Tina concluded. "No Coke,

even if he begs. And Loki's been fed, so don't let him con you, either.''

Henry came in through the kitchen door, stamping snow from his feet. He said: "Good morning, Mom. Take your breakfast into the living room—I started a fire for you. Well, the car's nice and warm. If we're picking up Tully, we'd better roll.''

His parents embraced Hen with admonitions to be good, and he nodded, his attention wholly fixed on "Tom and Jerry." They filed out, Tina saying over her shoulder: "The van comes for him at twelve-thirty. His clothes are on his bed.''

May's will. How extraordinary that the thought of it hadn't entered my mind before. Had it occurred to the others and they hadn't mentioned it because it might appear calculating? I certainly had no expectations from May. Had Sadd? Had Henry? Had Jon? We'd all been out of touch with her until recently, and surely the will was long since made? And she had not expected to die yesterday, of that I was certain.

Loki wandered in and brushed my leg, then circled back and rested against the old bathrobe almost as if he recognized it. I picked him up and walked into the living room. The fire was crackling, and I sat down, holding him in my lap like a great, lovely muff. How could I have left him? Then I reminded myself that he might not have survived the trip south, and Hen had begged for him. Yes, Loki was better off here, still so beautiful with his blue, near-blind eyes and glossy sable points. I wept over him a little, remembering how Henry Gamadge had loved this cat and loved holding him like this. . . .

The phone rang for the first time. By the fifth time, I had my spiel down pat. Might I ask if the *Times* had given out this number? Yes, this was the residence of

Mrs. Henry Gamadge who had called in the obituary, and I was Mrs. Gamadge, Senior. Yes, Mrs. Dawson was my cousin. No, I could only say how shockingly sudden . . . Yes, the services would be private, as indicated. Thank you for calling. Among the callers were several old friends. Was I back in New York for good? No, but I would be in a few months. Yes, I was enjoying Florida.

About mid-morning, daughter Paula called to beg that I come to Boston for a few days when all this was over. I said not now but certainly when I returned in April, and I urged her to go up and visit an elderly, lonely relative named Tully Hewitt in Gloucester. Paula replied that they often made day trips to the north shore and had she known she had a relative in Bass Rocks, she'd have sponged on him long since.

Between calls, I managed to get dressed, empty the dishwasher, hack something out of the freezer for supper, read to Hen, and finally get him into his van.

Then I sat down to make a phone call of my own.

10

AN ELDERLY MALE VOICE SAID: "HOLY MAR-
tyrs Cemetery. Cassidy speaking."

I told Mr. Cassidy my name and asked for directions
to Holy Martyrs from Brooklyn Heights. He gave them
to me with admirable exactitude.

"And is the office on the grounds?" I asked.

"Yes, that would be the second gate. If you're coming by bus, it's the corner of Montvale Avenue."

The thought of traveling to Queens by bus in January
made my blood run cold. "Are you open every day?"
I asked.

"The cemetery is. The office is closed on Sunday.
Are you inquiring about a burial?"

"No, I'm interested in one of the mausoleums. The
Dawson mausoleum."

There was a pause. Mr. Cassidy's voice became a
shade less brisk. "There seems to be quite a bit of
interest in that place lately. Somebody was out here a
week ago asking about it."

"So I understand. I'm a member of the family, by
the way."

"I told Mrs. Dawson about it when she came out
here to say that Mr. Lloyd Cavanaugh was dying and
we might be opening."

"Yes, she mentioned it. You don't know who it was—

the person who was asking, I mean. You didn't get his name?''

"It was a woman."

As the kids say—YIKES!

"I also told Mrs. Dawson"—Mr. Cassidy's voice took on a kind of resignation—"that Mrs. Lloyd Cavanaugh probably had other plans for her husband."

I said: "Mrs. Dawson herself died yesterday, very suddenly."

"I know." Resignation was now complete. "I thought perhaps that's why you were calling, but I was pretty sure she'd go elsewhere."

Elsewhere. Always elsewhere. An image if the "ugly, vulgar pile of marble," as Tully had described it, rose in my mind, and possibly in Mr. Cassidy's. He said: "What is your particular interest in the place, Mrs. Gamadge?"

"Well," I said, glad of the chance to use the speech I'd rehearsed, "my maiden name was Dawson. James Cavanaugh, who, I'm told, built the mausoleum, used our name instead of his own, and I'm curious to know why."

I wasn't the only one who was rehearsed. Mr. Cassidy's reply was as smooth as the lines of an actor in a long-running play: "Mr. Cavanaugh was connected through his brother Martin to the Dawson family, which he greatly admired. As I understand it, this was his way of honoring the family and providing a resting place worthy of them."

I said, and meant it: "How fascinating. And I feel so fortunate that I had a chance to speak with you, Mr. Cassidy. Have you been with Holy Martyrs long?"

"Since I was fourteen."

"Fourteen!"

Now the voice rang with pride. "I started as a gar-

72

dener back in the twenties. Cardinal Hayes got me in—he knew my dad. I was a grave digger till ten years ago.''

"What a fine career." I felt genuine admiration for Mr. Cassidy. "I'd love to meet you and chat more. I definitely plan a trip to Holy Martyrs. I've never seen the Dawson Mausoleum. By the way, would it be possible to go inside it?''

Mr. Cassidy was back to brisk. "We prefer not to open except for a burial. Our maintenance people don't have keys to the vaults, and we ask that wreaths and flowers and such be placed at the grille door.''

I assured Mr. Cassidy that any tribute I might want to lay on the tomb of James Cavanaugh would be placed at the grille door. We said good-bye.

Hummm. A woman.

The troops returned from White Plains, sans Jon and Tully, about four o'clock, just as Hen's van pulled up. It was good to be back to our original group. Tina produced marshmallows, and Hen sprawled before the fire, making a mess, as we sat with drinks and they described May's "service," apparently a rather bleak and peremptory affair. Sadd looked downright depressed, which surprised me, considering his often-voiced objections to what he calls "the funeral circus." He said:

"I couldn't help thinking of last night and the outpouring for Lloyd. There's something to be said for those old-fashioned going-away parties.''

"But a recluse is a tough person to throw a wake for," said Tina.

"Henry," I said, "what's the story on May's will?"

"I'll have it tomorrow. I called Bob McCloud on our way home."

I said, pulling Loki away from the toasting fork:

73

"I made a phone call myself today—rather an interesting one."

They looked at me with gratifying anticipation. I recounted my conversation with Mr. Cassidy, ending dramatically: "And he said the person who'd been out there asking questions was a *woman*!"

Sadd sat up, Henry grinned, and Tina looked sheepish. She said: "Don't get your hopes up. It was me."

Our burst of laughter sent Loki under the sofa. I spanked Tina as she bent over Hen. "Wretched girl! Why didn't you tell us you'd been to Holy Martyrs?"

"I honestly meant to, Clara"—she was pulling marshmallow from Hen's hair—"but it was the day before May crashed and with everything that's happened, I forgot to."

"Tell us now," said Sadd. "We've never seen the place. What's it like?"

"Incredible." Tina settled down beside Hen to prevent further depredations to the rug. "I'd been curious about Holy Martyrs ever since May described it to us, so I hied myself out there. Really, you have to see it to believe it. Acres and acres of stone monuments. It looks like an Edward Gorey set. According to Mr. Cassidy—who wasn't one bit happy about my questions—the cemetery was opened back in the eighteen-eighties. You simply don't believe such a place still exists—especially in the middle of New York."

Sadd leaned forward. "Did you see the Dawson mausoleum?"

"No, damn it, I couldn't find the place." Tina ran her hands through her hair in what I'd come to recognize as a gesture of frustration. "Here's what happened: First, I went to the office and told Mr. Cassidy some tale about how I'd just been to a burial near the Dawson mausoleum and somebody had told me about only one person being buried there and it made me curious. Well, Mr. Cassidy got very huffy and said there was nothing unusual about that because people often used to build those mausoleums and then the family died out or moved away—''

''—or hated them,'' from Henry.

''—or hated them, which I thought but didn't say, and then I asked Mr. Cassidy, who was the one person buried there? and he said it was James Cavanaugh, a wealthy contractor—''

''—and bootlegger—'' We were a Greek chorus.

''—and I didn't dare pump him any more or ask how to get to the place—I'd just faked being there—so I started to drive around that cemetery and there was my mistake. It's mammoth. Finally, I had to give up because Hen was due home from school.''

Tina put a marshmallow in her mouth and added: ''So you guys will just have to go out there and find the family monstrosity.''

I said: ''We're lucky. We don't need Mr. Cassidy. We have Martin. Sadd, did you make that phone call to Father Dever?''

Sadd snapped his fingers and stood up. ''What's the name of his church?''

''St. Agnes, in Hollis.''

''That should do it. Shall we take Martin to lunch tomorrow—that is, if his social calendar permits?''

''Absolutely.''

''Tell him not to dress,'' called Henry, as Sadd trotted off.

Tina said: ''You can use my car. But I should warn you—more snow is forecast.''

I quailed. ''Don't tell Sadd. He might back out. Henry, come with us. Don't you want to see Holy Martyrs?''

75

"Mom"—Henry piled glasses together—"if I don't get into the office tomorrow, I'll be a candidate for Holy Martyrs myself, meaning I'm *dead*."

He departed for his study, Tina dragged Hen off to the bathtub, and Loki emerged from under the sofa and indicated that we were alone. I picked him up and fed him a wheat cracker from the hors d'oeuvre tray; he had acquired a passion for them since belonging to Hen. I stared into the fire, envisioning again the echoing tomb of James Cavanaugh with my name large upon it. I wondered if my parents, who died of influenza when I was two, had contributed to the attitude that caused the vengeful use of their name. I hoped not. How passé that kind of snobbishness seemed now.

Sadd returned, waving a piece of paper. Father Dever was a peach. Anybody who took an interest in poor Marty Cavanaugh was a saint. Marty had no phone—one got the impression that possibly Marty had no home—but the good Father would see to it that Marty would be at St. Agnes's rectory at noon tomorrow, spruced up and ready for a visit from his kind relatives from Florida. And here was the good part: Holy Martyrs Cemetery, which figured prominently in the driving directions, appeared to be no distance at all from St. Agnes.

"So we take Marty out to lunch"—Sadd sat down and stretched his legs—"then do some sightseeing. One thing we're certain of: He knows his way to the revered resting place. Let's hope he's wearing all his jewelry."

"Sadd"—I'd only been half listening—"answer me honestly: Is Tully right? Will we be out of line going into that mausoleum tomorrow? Suppose some cemetery guard—I mean—we'd look like a pair of idiots or worse—"

"It occurred to me." Sadd beat Loki to the last wheat

cracker. "But to use your own phrase, the place does belong to us. And our advanced age adds innocence. We're a pair of eccentric oldsters reliving our past, remembering the days of Jim Cavanaugh and the speakeasies—"

I was giggling now.

"—and undoubtedly the great piles of snow, which I'm sure border all approaches to the mausoleum, will shield us nicely in the search for our roots."

"All right, all right. Answer me one more thing: Why do you suppose Martin goes in there?"

Sadd shrugged. "Probably some sort of morbid death wish. Father Dever says he's close to the DTs. And speaking of death wishes, I hope you've accepted the fact that May's was the result of that letter."

I hadn't, but I said I supposed so.

"Good. May she rest in peace."

The phone rang and was answered in the kitchen. Sadd went on: "Shouldn't we be making plans to return to a more civilized climate? How about the day after tomorrow? Surely you've had enough of this lovely weather."

No, Sadd, it wasn't the letter that killed poor May. It was the letter writer.

Tina appeared. "That was Mr. Lighter on the phone, May's lawyer."

Sadd said, yawning: "In the words of Mr. Stiggins, 'has she left me any small token?' "

Tina smiled. "No, she left everything to a fund called Children and Hunger. The portrait of Ellen goes to Tully, and there was one bequest: fifty thousand dollars to Jon. You'll never hear the end of the chanting now, Sadd. Supper's ready."

11

THE SNOW WAS DESULTORY AND THE SUN
holding its own when Sadd stopped the car before an
enormous, old, red-brick church in a congested area of
Hollis. Steep steps led straight up from the street and
were topped by a statue of a pious-looking young lady
holding a lily and pointing to her heart.

"St. Agnes, no doubt." Sadd turned off the ignition.
I'm always relieved when Sadd turns off the ignition.
His driving is erratic, and snow promotes it to hair-
raising. "And stop implying that I'm jealous of Jon."

"I'm not implying anything." Actually, I was pre-
occupied with another aspect of Jon's good fortune.

"I don't need the money"—Sadd pulled off gloves—
"though it's always nice to get. And of course, Jon will
blow it on more arty caterwauling."

"Really, Sadd, you sound like Archie Bunker."

"I suppose I do. What's that creature trying to tell
us?"

A gnomish figure brandished the broom with which
he was sweeping the church steps.

"I think he's pointing." Our eyes traveled to a sign
across the street, CHURCH PARKING. I said, as Sadd
started the car again, "I wonder if May had told Jon or
will it come as a lovely surprise."

"He said when she made her first donation she promised him more.'' With what could only have been the protection of St. Agnes, Sadd got us parked between a school bus and a snowbank. ''Why do you ask? Are you casting Jon as May's murderer? I thought you'd given that stuff up.''

''I'm casting him as somebody she might have told about reopening the Ellen thing. They appeared to have been in touch lately.''

''Never thought of that. Let's ask him.''

I squeezed myself out of the car and into the eighteen inches he'd left me, yanked the door from the snowbank, and crossly demanded the one pair of gloves we had between us. Sadd yielded them reluctantly, said something about the stores being always open and I said yes, and why didn't he avail himself of them, and we walked across the street. The gnome had reached the bottom step in his sweeping. He said:

''Might you be the visitors Father Dever is expecting?''

''We might that,'' said Sadd in a bad brogue.

''The rectory's in the back. Down Le Roy Street there, first door.''

No, Jon could not have been a threat to May. He was too guileless. Hints, possibly flattery, would be his only weapons, and early fulfillment of hopes just a dazzling surprise.

We were upon the sanded steps that led to the door marked RECTORY. Sadd stopped, skidding a little on a bare sliver.

''If you're thinking Jon may have written the anonymous letter—''

''Don't be absurd. Ring the bell—I'm cold.''

But the door opened, and there stood a white-haired, smiling Victor McLaglen in a clerical collar.

''And this would be Mrs. Gamadge and Mr. Saddlier. I'm Father Dever. Come in, come in, we're all delighted.''

It wasn't a brogue in the strict sense but the marvelous inflection of the educated Irish. I could listen to it forever. But—''*all* delighted''? Not ''both''? Who besides himself and Martin could be there and be delighted? We were stamping off snow and being relieved of coats, and Father Dever was talking about a place in Florida where he and his brother, a monsignor in Syracuse, were considering buying for their retirement. Now we entered a spanking clean parlor where sat Martin, his hair combed, beneath a picture of a bishop. On a horsehair sofa sat another man, Martin's age, with white and crêpey skin, as stiff and gimlet-eyed as Martin was hunched and rheumy.

Father Dever said: ''Mrs. Gamadge, you've met this gentleman—on the phone, at least—Frank Cassidy. He's with Holy Martyrs Cemetery. He was kind enough to drive Marty here. And this is Mr. Saddlier, Frank.''

If Mr. Cassidy was delighted, he concealed it as he rose and shook hands with us. Then he sat down again and looked even less delighted. I smiled at Martin, who did not rise but who managed to extract a hand from the grubby folds of his coat and surrender it to us. Then I nodded brightly at Mr. Cassidy.

''Why, of course! Mr. Cassidy and I had such a nice chat yesterday. What a pleasant coincidence that he knows you, Martin.''

Martin did not vouchsafe a reply, and Father Dever said: ''They're by way of being related, Mrs. Gamadge. As am I. You see before you three persons with a common grandmother—or is it grandfather, Frank? I never get it right.''

I said merrily: ''Perhaps all five of us are related! I was a Dawson and they're related to the Cavanaughs.''

"And the Saddliers are related to the Dawsons," cried Sadd.

"So this could very well be a family reunion," I chirped.

Father Dever slapped his knee. "A cause for celebration!"

He rose and went to the door calling "Rosie, please!" We were a weird party: three of us chatty and relaxed, the other two silent and blank-faced. A stout woman appeared, and Father Dever asked her to bring sherry. The lopsided jollity continued as he returned to his seat, sat forward, his great hands on his knees, and beamed about.

"Now, let's try to figure this out: Which of us is his own grandpaw?"

Sadd laughed with what I knew was genuine appreciation. He said: "I love this sort of thing. Take your name, for instance, Father. How do the Devers connect with, say, the Cavanaughs?"

"It's all a multicousinship, Mr. Saddlier." The giant priest leaned back and stretched his legs. "A cousin of mine, Maura Dever, a lovely girl, married James Cavanaugh, a thorough-going rascal. You may know of him."

"Vaguely, vaguely," said Sadd.

"Mrs. Gamadge knows of him." Mr. Cassidy spoke suddenly and clearly.

"Yes, indeed." I was proud of my quick nod. "We had a chat about his mausoleum yesterday."

"Oh, that dreadful place!" Father Dever threw up his hands. "Should be torn down."

Mr. Cassidy spoke again, defensively. "That was a real showplace once. Styles change, that's all. Do you know what it would cost to build it today?"

"Do you know anybody who'd *want* to build it today?'' Father Dever laughed and touched the man's thin arm. "Frank's a real company man. Every piece of crumbling cement in Holy Martyrs is dear to him.''

"It's very understandable," I said. "I was impressed when he told me he'd given his whole life to it.''

My little encomium did not cause Mr. Cassidy to look upon me more favorably. He stared at the floor and said:

"I don't want people thinking there's something wrong with the mausoleum. That kind of thing reflects on Holy Martyrs—all those stories about why Jim Cavanaugh is the only one buried there. He's the only one because his brother Martin wanted to be buried in Massachusetts in his wife's family plot and his brother Lloyd went out to Ohio and started a family there, and his wife, Maura"—his voice faltered here—"she wanted to be buried in Ireland—''

"Where she'd gone to die of drink, poor lamb.'' Father Dever's hand was still on the thin arm. "Frank, Frank, there's no use trying to whitewash—''

"I won't have Holy Martyrs made to sound like someplace in a cheapo thriller! Every inch of it is consecrated ground—''

"What interests me also—and forgive me for interrupting you, Mr. Cassidy"—Sadd was master of the tactful interruption—"is the Cassidy-Cavanaugh connection. I'm a genealogy buff, and my curiosity is thoroughly aroused.''

"Let's see . . .'' Father Dever looked at Martin with the encouraging smile of a good host. "Can you sort that out, Marty?''

Martin opened his mouth, shut it again, and fixed his eyes on the door. Footsteps in the hall—surely the tread of angels, his face seemed to say—heralded the arrival of the sherry. Father Dever took the tray from Rosie and put it on the coffee table, saying matter-of-factly: "One glass, Marty."

The sherry was poured and passed, Sadd and I accepted it, Martin seized it, and Frank Cassidy declined it. Father Dever sat back, sipped his, looked from the Cavanaugh to the Cassidy contingent, and apparently decided that the conversation was more likely to flourish in the hands of the latter.

"Frank," he said, "you'd best untangle it for Mr. Saddlier."

Mr. Cassidy said he'd changed his mind and would like some sherry after all. It was poured, and he said, not drinking it:

"Maura Dever was my half sister. Her father died and her mother married my father. Maura was the oldest of the first family and I was the youngest of the second, so she was really more like a half mother. When Maura married Jim Cavanaugh and came to this country, she brought me with her. That was in 1924. I was eleven and she was twenty-five. I remember how happy she was to see some other Devers, Father's family. They lived in Yonkers."

"We'd been starving in Ireland," said the priest cheerfully, "so our branch had piled over right after the first war."

Mr. Cassidy wet his lips with the sherry and went on: "Now, there were at the time of Jim's arrival back in the States relatives of his living in Flatbush—"

My head swam a bit. Where had I heard that cadence, that phrasing . . . "there were at that time shepherds keeping their flock in Flatbush"? Were all the Irish poetical in spite of themselves?

"—the family of Jim's brother, Martin. A fine, big family. Marty here was the youngest. He and I became friends."

83

Martin nodded and put his empty glass imploringly back on the tray. Father Dever said: "I remember such pleasant times at the Cavanaugh summer place in Patchogue the summer I was ordained—"

He stopped suddenly and sat upright, a startled look on his big, kind face. "Dawson," he said, looking at me, "you said your name was Dawson. The lady who died in New York just the other day—the mother of that lost girl—was she related to you?"

"My aunt," I said.

There was an instant of silence, then Father Dever put his hands on the arm of his chair and pushed himself to his feet. He said: "Excuse me a moment, please."

He went out. Sadd moved slightly, but I couldn't risk looking at him. I said: "Mr. Cassidy, did you know Ellen?"

"I saw her once or twice that summer. And I know the case, of course."

"Did Ellen die?" emerged from Martin.

Sadd said: "Martin, where would you like to go for lunch? We'll have to leave it in your hands. We don't know the area."

The concept that Martin would "know the area" relative to civilized lunching caused a strangled feeling in my throat. But he was not without a useful preference. He said: "Chinese."

"Good," said Sadd. "Love the stuff myself."

Father Dever came back into the room holding an envelope; it took no prescience to know what it contained. He said, standing in the midst of us:

"I received this letter about two weeks ago, and it upset me greatly. When I heard the poor lady had died, I could only see it as the good Lord sparing her more pain." He pulled the letter from its envelope and extended it to me. "Will you read it aloud, Mrs. Gamadge?"

I took it and looked at the signature and said, clearing my throat, which was dry: "It's signed 'May Dawson.' "

"Dear Father Dever:

"You are probably wondering who I am and why I am writing to you. Think back to the summer of 1938 when the Martin Cavanaugh family attended your ordination. With them was a young girl, my daughter Ellen Dawson, who was visiting them. Perhaps you heard that a year later she disappeared and was never found."

"Perhaps I heard!" Father Dever sank into his chair. "As if the whole country didn't hear! Excuse me—go on."

"I am approaching ninety years of age and have been taken with a great longing to try once more to trace my daughter. It is my intention to reopen the investigation and I am contacting everyone still living whom I can think of who knew or met her within a year of that time. Ellen spoke of meeting you and being impressed with the beautiful ceremony of your ordination. Might you remember speaking to her on any subject that could furnish a lead? I would welcome any information, any crumb . . ."

I handed the letter blindly back to him, and the kind man said:

"There now—you see—and I'm so sorry—but it's done to you just what it did to me. I wept. And how could I reply? While I was still puzzling—even thinking of going to see her to beg her not to—she was called to her reward. Well, I must admit I feel a bit better having shared this with you. I hope it hasn't upset you too much, Mrs. Gamadge.''

His great arm around my shoulder and Sadd's gentle hand-patting brought me up. Mr. Cassidy sat looking straight ahead, and Martin uttered only one word by way of consolation: ''Chinese.''

''Yes, we should be getting along.'' Sadd stood up and then we all did, and Mr. Cassidy said there was a place called Hong Kong Gardens about six blocks down on the right. Father Dever pulled Martin's coat up smartly and buttoned it under his chin, saying: ''Not too many mai tais, Marty,'' and we all went into the hall.

I said: ''We'll be glad to take Martin home since you were kind enough to bring him, Mr. Cassidy.''

In perfect tandem, he and Father Dever said no, no, just bring him back to the rectory, and if their words weren't identical, their message was: Martin's digs were either unmentionable or inaccessible. Fine with me. I didn't relish the prospect of Sadd barging about in the snow looking for a Tom-All-Alone. We maneuvered Martin down the steps and around the corner. As he and I stood waiting for Sadd to pry the car loose, Martin waxed positively chatty. He said:

''I usually have a beer with lunch.''

But we weren't going to risk disgrace while Martin was in our custody. Besides, he would need his wits about him. I'd glimpsed an inch of string at his neck, so I knew he was prime for the sortie. But I felt like a lousy hostess when Martin repeated wistfully over chow mein:

''I usually have a beer with lunch.''

''So do I,'' said Sadd, ''but this hot tea tastes so

good on a cold day like today, I think I'll stick with it."

"Me too," I piped. "Have some of this pork, Martin, it's delicious."

"By the way"—Sadd heaped food on Martin's plate— "Mrs. Gamadge and I are very curious to see the Dawson mausoleum. Aren't we fairly near Holy Martyrs?"

"We sure are."

"Will you be our guide?"

"Sure I will." He brightened a little, and it broke my heart. Maybe one beer? Besides, the shaky hand with which Martin poured tea made me wonder if after lunch he might ask to be excused in order to head home to the source. Sadd would probably murder me, having heroically passed up the drink I knew he wanted, but he shouldn't have one anyway in view of the impending tour through the snowy canyons of Holy Martyrs.

I said: "I believe I'll have a beer after all. Will you join me, Martin?"

The aurora borealis was nothing compared to Martin's face. I ignored Sadd's glare.

12

TINA WAS RIGHT.

Holy Martyrs had to be seen to be believed. Even from the expressway, the prospect was surreal, especially with the thousands of monuments crusted with snow giving the impression of a marble forest.

The sun went under as we drove through the gate—one of six, Martin said—and into a vast preserve where every symbol of Christian consolation met the eye, numberless stone angels looked homeward toward Brooklyn, and granite saints galore pointed to a smoggy horizon.

"Drive straight ahead till I tell you." Martin leaned forward and breathed fragrantly on my neck. Whether from enforced sobriety or the excitement of the jaunt, he'd become increasingly talkative as we approached the sacred premises. Sadd, thanks perhaps to the Chinese tea, now maneuvered the narrow, not perfectly plowed roads extremely well, squeezing past oncoming cars and edging around mourners on foot. He said:

"This is a Siberian maze! Martin, how can you possibly know where you're going?"

"I have Maura's poem." Martin took from his pocket a crumpled paper. "I kind of know it by heart, but I've never been here in the snow before. Things look different. Here—you read it, Mrs. . . . ."

Whatever your name is. I took the paper and held it to the poor light of the window. Sadd peered out of his and said:

"The paths are named. This one is . . . St. Ignatius."

"Good." Martin actually bounced a bit. "Only two more to St. Ambrose."

I read the smudged, penciled words aloud:

Left on St. Ambrose, right on St. John
Cross St. Peter, then go right on
Till you come to Lazarus wearing a crown
Turn left on St. Joachim and Dawson you've found!

"Wonderful!" Sadd chuckled. "Sounds healthily male-dominated. Here we are at St. Ambrose, where we hang a left. Did Maura Cavanaugh write it? The girl was a dream."

"She was an angel."

I shivered. How many angelic girls had crossed Jim Cavanaugh's path? I said:

"Then Maura knew about the mausoleum before she—she went back to Ireland?"

"Oh, sure. She used to come out here and watch while it was being built. She said it was the ugliest thing in the United States of America."

"Whoops!—right on St. John!" Sadd made a sudden turn, and we lurched around a corner to where the road wound between increasingly bigger monuments and what looked like small houses.

"The vaults begin here," said Martin.

"What's the difference between a vault and a mausoleum?" I asked.

"Just size," said Martin. "The mausoleums are the biggies."

We moved along between higher and higher snow-banks. The day was growing grayer.

"Martin," I said, laying some groundwork, "you showed me a key to the Dawson mausoleum the other night. Do you have it with you?"

"I always have it with me."

"Do you suppose we could take a look inside?"

"Sure. Uncle Jim loves visitors. So do his buddies."

Sadd's hands tightened on the wheel. He said: "Tell us about these buddies. Who else besides you knows they're in there?"

"Cassidy."

"Frank Cassidy?" Sadd and I spoke as one, startled.

" 'Across St. Peter' "—Martin pointed ahead— " 'then go right on.' What comes next, Mrs. . . ."

"Er—'till you come to Lazarus wearing a crown.' "

Cassidy? Sadd was looking at me with a wild, questioning frown. I began to feel a little giddy. Oh, Henry Gamadge, oh, darling Henry, how you would have loved this!

"Is that Lazarus?" Sadd pointed to a corner monument. "Looks more as if he's wearing a cake."

Indeed, Lazarus's crown was topped by a glistening pile of snow frosting.

" 'Turn left on St. Joachim,' " chanted Martin, " 'and Dawson you've found!' "

"It may not scan," said Sadd, making the turn, "but it sure does the trick." He slowed to a stop.

DAWSON.

It's a creepy feeling to see one's name—even a former one—cut in great letters on a building that is notorious and despised. I was astonished by the size of the thing. It looked like a dwarf church, tower and all, humped, queer in shape, poor in design, the badly proportioned, stubby tower topped by a too big cross.

How could even that revered symbol, slightly tipped against the dull sky, manage to look ungodly?

I wasn't the only rapt gazer. Sadd had gotten out of the car and was leaning against the hood, transfixed. He said: "Aren't you glad you got married and changed your name?"

Martin, veteran visitor to the shrine, had no cause for contemplation. He'd scrambled out of the back seat and now stood looking at the bank of snow between himself and the door of the mausoleum. He called:

"Somebody's been here."

I didn't understand at first. Sadd and I walked up and looked at the deep prints sunk in the snow that led to the grille door.

Sadd said: "Jim Cavanaugh's had other visitors. Today."

"Jim never has visitors except me." It was almost a snarl. Martin scrambled into the bank and, dragging his heavy coat, hideously shiny and green against the snow, fought his way to the grille. He grasped the bars with both hands and stood rigidly looking in, then he called over his shoulder:

"Come on!"

Sadd and I looked at each other like a pair of old timers caught playing a game too young for us. I said:

"Department of broken hips. You first."

"Frankly, I don't think I can make it." Sadd stared at the stretch of snow, not more than fifteen feet, but it seemed like a frozen Sahara. "I doubt if I can get my knees that high. If I go down, you'll never get me up." He cupped his hands. "Martin, you can't get the door open against this snow. We'd better come back."

Something clicked in me. Let Henry Gamadge down? Never! I looked around. Not a soul, not a car, a condition devoutly to be wished for and perhaps not to be repeated. I plunged into the snow. It closed over the top of the short, chic boots Tina had loaned me, and I shrieked.

Sadd said: "Damn it, woman, you've shamed me!" He followed, singing, "I'm getting buried in the morning, ding dong the bells are gonna chime—and they can shove me right in with Uncle Jim!"

We arrived beside Martin gasping for breath, clung to the bars of the grille, and peered in.

The interior of the place was bathed in gloom, the only light a reddish ray from a high, begrimed, stained glass window. The concrete floor, between patches of drifting snow, was cracked and dirty. Facing us, in almost alarming proximity—not ten feet away—the rows of crypts piled up to an arch, not unlike drawers in a file cabinet, their slab fronts ungraven except one. Dead center, a dim inscription read JAMES CAVANAUGH, beloved something-or-other, and some dates.

Martin had sunk to his knees and was pushing snow from the bottom of the gate. Now he shook it as if imprisoned on the other side.

"It's padlocked! The bastard's padlocked it!"

A sound made us turn. A blue car rounded Lazarus and pulled up behind ours. Frank Cassidy got out. Martin galloped back across the snow yelling something. I began to giggle. When you giggle at the same time your teeth are chattering it produces an effect akin to a seizure.

Sadd said: "Better get hold of yourself, we are called on the carpet—oh, God, if only there was one!" And we floundered back to the road.

Mr. Cassidy, smiling steadily, even helping me brush snow from my coat, said: "I thought I might find you here. I'm sorry Marty had to disgrace himself in front of you nice folks."

The fact that you nice folks had disgraced yourselves in front of Marty was implicit. Martin stood silent and cowed. Whatever Frank had said to him, he was again the dim little mute who had sat in the rectory parlor.

Sadd said: "Mr. Cassidy, this was entirely our idea. At lunch we got to discussing the mausoleum, and since we were so near, we asked Martin—"

"Why, sure." Mr. Cassidy's smile was still firmly in place. "Mrs. Gamadge told me she was anxious to see it. I only wish you could be here in the spring. Holy Martyrs is a park—a real park, isn't it, Marty? Mr. Saddlier, I'm going to have to ask you to move your car—you were probably just about to leave anyway—there's a funeral procession coming any minute."

"A burial in this weather?" I said.

"Aboveground burials in any weather." Mr. Cassidy maneuvered around his smile, which hadn't budged. "Marty, why don't you hop in my car? It'll save these folks a trip back to the rectory."

Martin stood still, scowling at DAWSON. Did Cassidy sense a rebellious outburst? He added:

"I thought we might stop for a drink."

Foul! Foul! Martin scurried to the blue car, and Sadd, who afterward said he was silently reciting, "He who fights and runs away . . .," moved to ours. I stood my ground, hoping the funeral procession was an invention. I said:

"Martin was telling us a fascinating tale of skullduggery. Something about other people being buried in the mausoleum. How do you suppose such a story ever got started?"

"It got started when Marty got hooked on Jim Cavanaugh's bad booze." The smile didn't quite die, but it sickened a bit. "It began as Marty's pet joke and turned into a nightmare he believes in. Years ago, Marty used to help out in the office. That's how he got that key—which goes home with me today." The smiled expired. "Sorry, Mrs. Gamadge, but here's the procession."

A hearse was indeed approaching from across St. Joachim.

I said: "I'd love to hear more about all this someday. Perhaps you could—"

"Just follow me." Mr. Cassidy hurried to his car.

It was the one favor he did us. We'd have been wandering the labyrinthian ways of Holy Martyrs forever had Mr. Cassidy not led us to a gate, but not the one we had entered by, for we were soon lost again in the back streets of Hollis. When we stopped for gas and directions, we were reduced to gibbering exasperation.

Waiting for Sadd to return from the men's room, I slid determinedly over to the driver's seat. To my relief, when he appeared, bearing two cups of steaming coffee, he did not object and took up the conversation exactly where we'd left it.

"I just hope he doesn't beat up too hard on poor Marty."

"I just hope he buys him the drink he promised. Hold my coffee and give me the gloves." I drove the car around to the rear of the station and pulled up behind a tow truck.

"Don't turn the engine off"—Sadd handed back my coffee—"that heater is all that stands between us and death. Well, one thing is certain: Cassidy knows what Marty knows. And Tully was right. You don't have to get in there to realize those crypt fronts weigh a ton. Nobody could get them off without help. God, it's tantalizing! What's in there besides Jim?"

I said to myself . . . Ellen? But Sadd had told Henry

94

the thought was grotesque, and he wouldn't discuss it; in truth, it did seem beyond endurance. So I said lightly:

"Maybe it's gold bullion. Maybe it's—"

"Maybe it's time to get going. The kids will be sending out a search party. I think I'll call Father Dever in the morning and ask him more about it. What a nice guy—and no visible hang-ups."

But in the morning, it was Father Dever who called us. Martin had been found dead in bed.

13

I WAS GRATEFUL TINA WAS THERE.

Sadd literally had to be helped back to his chair at the kitchen table. I was pinned beneath Hen, who lay on my lap, listless with a cold. I doubt if I would have been able to move anyway, so stiff with horror was I when Sadd told me about Martin.

We'd been very merry at breakfast before Henry left, and then with Tina, relating the particulars of our mortifying rout from Holy Martyrs. Father Dever's call came at nine o'clock.

Tina poured a glass of sherry for Sadd and said: "How?"

"It seems he choked on his own vomit. Cassidy found him. There's to be a short service—a Mass—at Holy Martyrs chapel tomorrow and would we like to come. Martin will be stashed—you know where." Sadd gulped his sherry.

I heard myself say: "Cassidy killed him."

Tina stared. "You don't mean literally?"

"Sure she does." Sadd looked around dazedly. "Sure she does, and sure he did."

Tina moved impatiently. "Now, look you two—*quit it!* It's our fault. Henry and I have fed you with so many horrors, you're seeing spooks everywhere."

Hen wheezed, and she took him from my lap and

then looked from me to Sadd. "Damn it, much as I'd hate to lose you, I feel like putting the pair of you on a plane this morning—back to Florida and back to normal."

I vaguely heard her. Sadd was sitting motionless. Tina set Hen on his feet, sat down, and said pleadingly:

"Look: A poor drunk upchucks and chokes and dies; it happens all the time. Can't we go back to before May called us and forget she ever did? Forget Ellen. Forget Jim Cavanaugh. Be happy for Martin—he's gone to that big package store in the sky." She stood up. "I'm going to make more coffee."

Poor Tina. She didn't need this. I said:

"Thank you, dear, yes, I'd love another cup. And you're right—we should clear out. But not till tomorrow. We owe that to Martin. Can you stand us one more day? And we won't tie up your car again. We'll rent one and go straight from Holy Martyrs to the airport."

"Don't be an idiot." Tina made a great clatter at the sink. "Of course you'll take my car. Or rather, I'll take you in it." She turned. "Do you think I'd miss a chance to be at the opening of the Dawson mausoleum?"

Sadd grabbed her hand and kissed it. We all began to laugh and cry a little.

Mercifully, the weather turned warm next day, and the Long Island Expressway was merely a damp stretch. Even more mercifully, Tina was driving.

Sadd said: "I think I was on this expressway once before in my life. Now I've been on it three times in three days. Am I crazy?"

"Of course you are, we all are." I turned to look at him. "But think how nice it is to be wearing a dashing new cap and your very own pair of gloves."

I'd gone out shopping the afternoon before, partly to

97

clear my head, partly to get away from Sadd, who was all for turning Frank Cassidy over to the police at once. I'd taken a cab across the bridge and lost myself in Macy's for a few hours. It was lovely to wander about alone enjoying the bustle. I sat in the coffee shop and thought about poor Martin. No, Cassidy hadn't intentionally killed him, unless, of course, he'd deliberately engineered the binge that had done Martin in. Perhaps he hadn't even realized. . . . Perhaps just taking the key away was the last straw. Perhaps . . .

I returned to Willow Street, resplendent in a black, fake fur hat that Henry said made me look like Anna Karenina.

I said: "Thank you, dear. Well, maybe as Anna might have looked in forty years if she hadn't taken that dive."

We were at supper and I'd presented Sadd with a plaid cap and a pair of fur-lined gloves. He tried them on at once, pleased.

"But you can't soft soap me out of my killer." He tipped the cap at various angles. "Cassidy put a pillow on Martin's face or I'm not eating pie in gloves."

Henry said: "Be hard to prove, Sadd."

"No it wouldn't. What the hell was Cassidy doing at Martin's so early this morning? In fact, did he ever leave when he took Martin home? My guess is he got him loaded, stuck his finger down his throat, and sat on his head."

Tina gagged and said: "Might somebody have seen Cassidy come in with Martin—or seen him leave? Where does—did Martin live?"

"Who knows?" I stood up. "Evidently someplace too unlovely for us to see." I poured milk for Hen and tipped some into Loki's bowl.

Henry said: "Well, I'm jealous. You guys get to walk into that mausoleum tomorrow, and I'm stuck in court on a boring libel suit. By the way, I wonder which crypt will receive the remains of Martin. Who decides?''

Sadd said: ''The family, usually. But who's left?''

Tina said: ''Then probably Cassidy—Mr. Holy Martyrs himself.''

A thought occurred to me. ''I hope Father Dever has let Helen Cavanaugh know.''

''I'm sure he has.'' Sadd raised his new cap aloft. ''Here's to our third funeral in as many days. We're getting to be professional mourners.''

Dear God, it was a chilling fact. Mortality was rushing us. Even Loki seemed to me more feeble than usual as he sniffed his milk and decided wearily against it.

Sadd said: ''By the way, has anyone heard from Jon?''

''I called him yesterday to tell him his good news, but he wasn't home.'' Henry balanced Tina's apple pie on his palm. ''So I left a message on his answering machine to get back to me. Anybody want another piece of this?''

''I do.'' Sadd held out his plate.

Tina said, almost dreamily: ''Will Ellen's ghost cry out to us from one of the crypts?''

No one answered her; we seemed in silent agreement to treat the question as rhetorical. But it hung in my mind now as Tina, looking charming in a matching red wool cap and scarf, drove us along the expressway.

I said, looking at the clock on the dash: ''Is it really only nine-fifteen? I feel as if I've been awake for ten hours.''

''We're in quite a pattern, aren't we?'' said Sadd. ''Up at dawn to attend the day's obsequies.''

But his tone was weary as well as bantering. Was the whole thing too much for Sadd? The man was seventy-four. I was six years younger and already feeling rather punchy.

I said: "What time is our flight, Tina?"

"The best Henry could do was ten-twenty tomorrow morning. Sorry about this afternoon, but there just wasn't a thing."

A horn sounded behind us as Tina took a turn off the expressway. Sadd turned and said: "It's Helen Cavanaugh."

We all waved out our windows, and she waved back. I said:

"I'm so relieved! How much farther, Tina?"

"Almost there."

The chapel at Holy Martyrs was a small, bestatued edifice across the road from the office at the main gate. The snow was melting fast in the sunlight, and their white vestments were sliding from the shoulders of the monuments. On the chapel steps stood a short, heavy woman holding a little boy by the hand. The hearse was there, and Frank Cassidy was beside it. He signaled to us to pull ahead of it. We got out and waited for Helen Cavanaugh to join us.

She came up, shaking her head. "This is ghastly. You must think we do nothing here but die."

I said: "This is no picnic for you, Helen. Have you met Tina, Henry's wife?"

She had not, and we stood chatting, Sadd's eyes wandering to Cassidy, who was studiously avoiding us. The woman with the little boy came down the steps and walked toward us. Helen said quickly:

"This must be Mrs. Horan from Martin's housing project. I think she used to keep an eye on him. Mrs. Horan?"

The woman said yes and immediately started to talk.

"You'll be his folks. Father Dever said to be sure and speak to you. This is my grandson. His mother works."

"Mrs. Horan"—Sadd took her hand—"we're so grateful you came. Can you tell us what happened?"

"But tell us inside," I said, looking at the child's pink nose. We walked past the hearse with its shadowy burden and up the chapel steps, as Cassidy hurried across the road toward the office.

Sadd said: "Oh, no you don't!" and went after him. I thought, good for you, Sadd. He'd promised he wouldn't say anything wildly accusatory, but Frank Cassidy was not to be allowed to look through us. The rest of us entered the chapel. It was only slightly warm, empty, and not yet lighted. We groped our way into the back pew.

Tina whispered to the child: "I just remembered something in my car you might like. Come get it with me."

They went out again, and Mrs. Horan, ensconced between Helen and me, began to enjoy herself in a loud whisper.

"Any day—that's what I've been saying to my husband—any day. And he'd vomited before, I know that. So it came as no surprise, no surprise at all."

I said: "When did you last see Martin?"

"Let's see . . ." Mrs. Horan frowned like a witness on Perry Mason—"I guess it was the day before yesterday. I seen him in the morning. Then I heard him talking to Mr. Cassidy in the hall around noon and then around five o'clock. I figured they'd been somewheres. I didn't look in on him that night. My husband don't like me going in the hall after dark. There was a stabbing on our floor last month. Then later, I heard Mr. Cassidy leave."

"You didn't *see* him leave?" I wondered if Helen thought the question odd, but she only said:

"Then he must have gone back. Father Dever said Mr. Cassidy found him in the morning."

Mrs. Horan nodded. "He probably just went out to get Martin some food, and then maybe he stayed all night. He did that sometimes. He was real good to Martin. I think they were related or something. They used to pal together before Martin's drinking got so bad. Anyways, yesterday morning Mr. Cassidy comes banging on my door and it's all over."

Tina reappeared, and we made room for her and the child in the pew. He was clutching a box of animal crackers.

Mrs. Horan whispered: "That's real nice of you."

"I have a little boy myself. I always keep something in the car for emergencies." Tina automatically assumed our respectful whisper. "Father Dever just arrived. I introduced myself. What a sweetheart. He said he wished Martin could have some music, but there isn't an organ in this chapel."

Mrs. Horan said: "You can bet on it, Father's paying for whatever this costs—including getting Martin buried in that awful place. We got a plot in Holy Martyrs ourselves. Martin showed me that mausoleum once. I hate them things. Give me God's good earth, I always say."

"Where's Sadd?" I asked Tina.

"He's talking to Mr. Cassidy and Father Dever."

We fell silent, sitting in the dimness; the only sound was the scrounging of small fingers in the cracker box. I had a sense of unreality. What was I doing sitting in a barely heated church, feet numb to the ankles, awaiting the remains of a pathetic creature whom I'd never heard of till this week? I wrenched my thoughts to Santa Martina Island, to a cove on its northernmost shore where Tampa Bay and the Gulf of Mexico merge in a beautiful and dangerous expanse of swirling water. The sun would be blinding, the gulls would be soaring. . . .

The lights in the chapel went on. A modest arch was revealed and a wedding cake of an altar. The doors behind us opened, and we rose to face the coffin advancing on its trolley—flanked by Sadd and Frank Cassidy!

I converted my gurgle—successfully, I hope—into a cough, and Tina grasped my arm, smothering a similar convulsion. Hired pallbearers cost money and Father Dever was nothing if not resourceful. Now he himself emerged from behind the altar, handsomely vested in black, and stood awaiting Martin's approach. The undertaker, a thin man and, as Tina later said, "the only other pro in the show," paced behind the two non-union members of the cast, guiding their progress.

But why did I also feel like weeping? Was it the great stretch of empty pews between us and Martin? True, Sadd and Cassidy were directed to take the front pew on either side, but the five of us remained frozen in the rear of the chapel as Father Dever began the Mass. And there was another emptiness . . . the utter silence, except for the low voice of the priest. I thought of Martin's words: "Lloyd said he'd bring me over to St. Bernard's and give me the whole works—choir and all." My sadness mounted as, under the assured guidance of Mrs. Horan and Helen, we stood, sat, and knelt. At one point, the door behind us opened and closed, but no one joined us. Evidently a devotional visitor, perceiving a funeral in progress, had hastily backed out.

Now the Mass was over.

The undertaker signaled to Sadd and Cassidy to resume their duties. As they began their slow procession toward us, suddenly, heartrendingly, Martin got his wish.

A fine baritone voice began to sing "Ave Maria."
Jon!

It was so stunning, so unexpected, so wonderful. We turned, bumping into each other, gawking at Jon, who stood, unwrapping a scarf from his neck and making the arch ring with the hymn which, at least momentarily, is the downfall of doubters, the confusion of agnostics, and, in this case, almost the undoing of Sadd and Cassidy, who advanced with streaming faces and wavering steps. Our back-pew delegation smiled weepily as the glorious *a cappella* soared to a climax and the coffin reached the door.

It was easy to imagine Martin already wafted to cloud *cum* harp.

14

IN THE CAR, AS WE FOLLOWED THE WINDING route of the hearse, I leaned into the front seat and hugged Jon. Sadd slapped his back, and Tina said:

"Jon, that was just plain wonderful."

"That was just plain lucky." He laughed, pleased with our pleasure. "I didn't turn on my answering machine till this morning, and then I just caught Henry as he was leaving for court. Poor Marty! He used to love those requiem High Masses at St. Bernard's. When I saw that dim little chapel and that no-frills Mass!"

"And that crowd of mourners!" Tina laughed. "All seven of us, including Mrs. Horan's grandson." She braked suddenly. "My God—I forgot them! Should I have waited for them?"

"Not to worry," I said. "Father Dever sent them home in a cab."

"And Helen Cavanaugh's left," said Sadd. "She's had all she can take, poor thing."

"This place is incredible." Jon peered out of the window. "Aunt May told me about it once—something about just one person being buried—" He stopped and looked shyly from one to the other of us. "Did Henry tell you?"

I said: "Yes, dear. I'm so glad May did that."

"We're delighted for you, son."

Tina said: "It's great, Jon."

"Thanks, Tina. Did you ever meet Aunt May?"

The question, so sudden, so innocent, so revealing, reduced us all to silence for a few seconds. Fortunately, a horn sounded behind us. Frank Cassidy, Father Dever seated beside him, was signaling to us from his car. Tina stopped, and he got out and hurried to her window. He said:

"When the hearse stops, pull up *behind* it. It will have to leave before we do."

Tina nodded and moved on.

So May had said nothing to Jon? Did he even know of Ellen's existence? He could only have heard of her from his father. In the front seat, Jon was asking Tina about probate. I said quietly to Sadd:

"He may never have heard of Ellen. Did you ever discuss the case with him?"

"Never."

Then that was that. But . . . the portrait in May's living room. Surely Jon had sat there, had seen it.

I said: "Speaking of wills, isn't it nice that the portrait of May's daughter goes to Tully. Did you ever see it, Jon?"

He nodded and turned. "Yes, the first time I went to Aunt May's apartment. I asked her who it was, and she said it was her daughter and that they had 'lost her.' I suppose people can't bear to say 'die' when they refer to a child, especially their own."

Sadd said: "Here's Lazarus wearing his crown. We're almost there."

"I didn't know you'd ever been here, Dad."

"I practically live here," said Sadd, and Tina laughed at Jon's bewilderment and said it was a tale for around the fire someday. She pulled up behind the hearse and we got out.

106

Uglier than ever, the veil of snow gone from its roof, DAWSON loomed to receive Martin. Two workmen were shoveling a path to the door, and now one of them swung open the grille. I thought fleetingly of Martin plunging through the drifts, our trespassing footsteps following after. It had been more fun than the tame scene that now ensued as the workmen carried him up the path and set his coffin down just inside the mausoleum. Then they walked away, shovels over shoulders.

The undertaker got back into the hearse, and it pulled away.

We stood uncertainly in the road. Father Dever and Frank Cassidy were standing beside their car, earnestly talking. Or was Father doing the talking?

From inside the mausoleum came a pattering sound. We looked at each other, then with one accord, walked up the path to the door.

A young workman stood on a ladder scraping bits of mortar from the yawning cavity of the topmost left crypt. Its slab lay on the ground. Jon said softly, as we all stared in:

"I could hardly believe it when May told me, but sure enough there's the one inscription. What a bastard he must have been."

The workman turned and nodded to us. He said: "Mr. Cassidy here yet?"

"Right behind us," said Sadd.

Tina said: "Who decides who goes where?"

The workman shrugged. "Mr. Cassidy told me to open this one. Plenty of choice." He laughed and tossed a pebble at Jim Cavanaugh. "That dude's finally got company."

Sadd said: "I wonder if we're expected to give Martin a leg up."

"Oh, he won't be placed till this afternoon, maybe tomorrow. The mason has to be here to seal the slab."

I looked at it. "There's no inscription."

"That costs." The boy jumped down from his ladder and collected his tools. "Some people don't bother. Well, see you." And the lively young worker among the dead went off whistling.

We stood there glumly. Tina said:

"If Martin doesn't get 'placed' now, why are we here?"

"A few more prayers, I guess," said Jon.

Father Dever and Frank Cassidy were approaching the path. I walked around Martin's coffin to the bank of crypts and looked up at them. The huge slab fronts, though not sealed, appeared to be firmly in place. Oddly, the only one that looked loose was Jim's own. The mortar had been chipped away in spots, and the slab jutted and sagged slightly.

I said: "If any of Jim's buddies are here, I'd say they'd have to be right in his own crypt with him."

"They are, Mrs. Gamadge."

It was Frank Cassidy's voice. We all agreed later that the words didn't register at once. I was aware that Father Dever looked bigger than ever in a bright blue parka, his thick, white hair blowing. His only vestment was a narrow, purple satin stole with a cross at each end. He held a prayer book, and Cassidy carried a small bag. I recall walking back to the door and standing with the others as the priest opened his prayer book and said cheerfully:

"We'll give Marty the final blessing that will commend him to the Lord. Then Frank and I have something to show you."

He began to read. At one point, we were requested to recite The Lord's Prayer and I suppose we got through

108

it. Father Dever closed his book and helped Cassidy cover the coffin with a purple pall. Then he said:

"I don't want you folks to catch cold. We'll be as quick as possible. When Frank has the slab free, I think, among us, we can lift it off."

Cassidy snapped open a brown plastic bag. Next came a hammer. He started to chip at the crumbling mortar on Jim Cavanaugh's crypt.

Father Dever went on: "When the mason comes the slab will be back in place, and he'll be told it had come loose and should be re-sealed. Because what we do here is in confidence, of course. We're all members of the family one way or another, and this place has been a shadow on us too long."

A few more ringing blows, and Cassidy threw down his tools. Then the three old men and the single young one grasped sides and corners of the tipsy slab and, amid a shower of mortar fragments, staggered back with it.

The bottles, stacked against the moulding coffin, winked at us evilly. Frank Cassidy lifted out an ugly greenish quart that gurgled in his hand. He said:

"Care for a swig? Jim Cavanaugh's special brew. Very old stock."

On the phone, Tina was assured by Teresita that Hen's cold was better, but he'd been asking when his mother was coming home, and that sent her flying to her car. Jon, an audition scheduled for one o'clock, asked to be dropped off at the nearest subway stop. I waved them off with assurances that we'd report in full and that Father Dever had offered us a ride back to Willow Street. Then I returned to the blessed warmth of the Hong Kong Gardens.

My whiskey sour had just arrived, and Sadd moved

over in the booth. We all raised our glasses in a toast to Martin.

"He was such a good-looking kid," said Father Dever. "Played fine baseball. How old was he when he got hooked, Frank?"

"About eighteen. Jim had him working in that warehouse of his out in Riverhead. Marty quit school to do it. The stuff was such poison. I had a fair amount of it myself. But Marty was like Maura, he couldn't handle it."

"He tried to quit in his middle years." The priest looked into his beer. "We all thought he'd licked it. Then he married Grace and she died and the baby died, and that cooked his goose." He smiled at me. "We've ordered for you, Mrs. Gamadge. It's your favorite, Mr. Saddlier said. Moogoo something."

"The day I learn to pronounce it," said Sadd, "I plan to open my own place."

Cassidy's hands toyed with his chopsticks, then threw them down. "I'd like to say something. I feel bad that you folks thought I was rude or whatever, but things had got so bad with Marty, I was scared he'd break into that place and start a scene and then there'd be a lot of rotten publicity. Recently, he'd been chipping away at the crypt to get at the stuff we put there the night Jim was buried."

Our lunch arrived, and for the first time in my life, I didn't dive immediately into my moogoo something. I said: "Could you tell us about it, Mr. Cassidy?"

"It was the first night of Jim's wake." He started instantly, almost like a dam bursting. "Those were the days of three-day wakes with open casket. Marty and I had been sitting there looking at Jim all painted up and his hair slicked down and the rosary beads wrapped around his hands, and Marty said he thought he was going to throw up.''

With the last words his face changed pathetically, and he looked at Sadd. ''And that's the way Marty died, Mr. Saddlier. He threw up, I swear he did.''

''Mr. Cassidy, I never doubted it.'' Sadd stuffed fried rice into his lying mouth.

Father Dever looked bewildered. He said: ''Why would anybody—''

''I just want them to know what happened. Mr. Saddlier was asking me about it this morning. I took Marty home after I'd bought him the drink I'd promised him— that was only fair—and when we got to his place I told him I wanted the key and he said no and he fought me for it and then he dives under the bed and comes up with a bottle and I went out to get some cold cuts and when I got back he was passed out. I didn't dare leave— I knew he'd vomited before—so I went to sleep in a chair, and when I woke up, Marty was dead. That's the God's honest truth.''

''Of course it is.'' Father Dever put his arm around the vibrating shoulder. ''Now eat. I'll tell about Jim's wake.''

''But you don't know—''

''Sure I do. You told me. You and Marty sat there admiring Jim and talking about Maura—she'd been dead about a year—and looking around at the measly bunch of relatives and big bunch of thugs, and Dan Flanagan, Jim's lawyer, came up to you and dropped the bomb: Jim had told him he was to have Maura's body—what's that word—'exhumed' from her grave in Ireland and brought over and buried next to him.''

Sadd said: ''I don't think that would hold up in court if the family didn't want—''

''We didn't and it didn't.'' Cassidy took up the story

111

warmly. "Marty and I hot-footed it to a telegraph office and got a message off to Maura's mother in Ireland—she was in her late eighties—telling her to stand by for this order and let Flanagan know what she thought of it. Later she wrote me she'd sent his letter back in twenty pieces. She was a great old lady."

"Great," I murmured, entranced.

"Anyway, Jim was buried a few days later. It was a Saturday—my twenty-fifth birthday, I remember—and Marty and I were doing some painting and plastering in the office of Holy Martyrs. We saw Jim's hearse go by around noon, and about four o'clock I said I sure could use a drink but it was cold and rainy and I didn't feel like going out. Marty said he could fix that, and he went out to his car and came back with a bag of bottles. I knew he'd hoarded some of Jim's stuff when Prohibition went out but my God, this was 1940 and that booze was ten, twelve years old and it was always filthy but now it was . . ."

"Lethal," breathed Sadd.

"And you never got so crazy drunk in your life," Father Dever opened a fortune cookie.

"What did it was, we got arguing about the color of Maura's hair. I said it was red and Marty said it was gold. And I said imagine putting her in with that scum and there wasn't anything bad enough to be buried with him and Marty looked at the bag of bottles and said yes there was."

The waitress brought the check, and Sadd and Father Dever both reached for it. Sadd won, which was rather remarkable considering that he never took his eyes off Frank Cassidy.

"We lugged the stuff out to Marty's car and God knows how we ever got to the mausoleum in one piece, but it was after five and the cemetery was closed. Marty

112

had his key and we walked into the place and the mortar was still wet around Jim's slab. We pulled it off and starting spitting on the bottles and throwing them in next to the coffin. Then we put the slab back and tamped the mortar back, and I hope that creepy bastard has been enjoying his company all these years.''

Father Dever read aloud the slip from his fortune cookie: '' 'You are a very kind and forgiving person.' I think I got yours by mistake, Frank.''

I blessed him for the laugh.

When they dropped us off in front of Nice Ugly and declined our invitation to come in, Sadd said, ''I have a rotten sore throat.''

15

"PETER WILL BE AWFULLY DISAPPOINTED, Sadd," said Henry. "Are you sure you can't come?"

"I tell you I'm at death's door. What's my temperature, Tina?"

"Normal."

"I don't believe it. It has to be a hundred and ten. I can't raise my head."

I said: "You just have a bad cold and you're exhausted. Stop feeling sorry for yourself. Feel sorry for Tina and Henry. They're stuck with us till you *can* raise your head."

"And my ass," groaned Sadd. "I'm sorry, you guys."

"Oh, shut up," said Tina.

We were all crowded into the little study, which I'd reluctantly surrendered as a "sickroom" when Sadd had announced his impending demise. Tina sat on the couch beside him, I had the desk chair, Hen lay on the floor with Loki on his stomach, and Henry leaned in the doorway. He said:

"I just hate for you to miss dinner at Othello's. The scampi is outstanding. Maybe we should be heroic and all decline."

"Not on your life," I said. "I'm not going to miss a

chance to talk to Peter Angier. I want to know if he got a letter from May. Or wrote her one.''

"You want the scampi," growled Sadd.

"That too."

Tina said: "When his wife called and said, 'This is Ruth Angier,' the name didn't register. Then she said, 'My husband Peter and I want to take you all out to dinner.' As the British say, I twigged."

"Don't mind me." Sadd turned over with a sigh. "Go and enjoy yourselves. Hen will keep me company. We'll ask each other riddles, like 'why did I ever leave Florida?' "

Loki assayed a leap to the couch but made it only to the edge, where his claws caught the quilt and it slid with him to the floor. Sadd groaned, and Tina hustled cat and son out of the room. "Hen will have had his supper," she called reassuringly, "and we'll bring you a doggie bag."

Henry took her place on the couch beside Sadd. He said: "Are you sure you feel up to baby-sitting?"

"Certainly, if the child doesn't require being read to or rocked." Sadd sat up and blew his nose. "Clara, what do you propose to say to Peter Angier? His wife may know nothing about the case. He only married her about ten years ago."

"If you're trying to tell me not to be tactless, I'll do my best."

"I only meant—"

"I don't plan to say, over the fruit cup, 'By the way, Mrs. Angier, did you know that your husband was once involved in a tragedy and never fully cleared?' "

"Yes he was, Mrs. Smarty."

"Actually, he wasn't, Sadd," said Henry. "Neither were the other kids. That is, their statements couldn't be proved or disproved. It was always rather a shadow on them. Peter's the only one still living.'' We were silent for a minute, then Henry added: ''Sadd's got a point, Mom. It could be ticklish.''

Sadd said: ''All you have to do is arrange for Mrs. A. to be locked in the ladies' room for about twenty minutes. I assume you don't plan to interrogate him all evening.''

''I just want to know if May wrote to him and—''

''Of course she did, if she wrote to someone as remote as Father Dever.''

''—and I want to know if he replied—anonymously or otherwise—and I want to know if he went to see her.''

''Would you expect him to tell you that?''

''Why not, if he has nothing to hide?''

Henry had been looking from me to Sadd. ''What are you two talking about? 'Went to see her'? 'Nothing to hide'? Do you know something I don't know?''

''Your mother''—Sadd slid down on his pillows—''is behaving in true Gamadge fashion—seeing suspects everywhere. Why don't you question the cat, Clara? Perhaps May wrote to him. Henry, you'd better watch this woman at dinner tonight if you want Peter to pick up the check. Now these are my last words: Which of you is going to get me a bourbon?''

''I am,'' said Henry and went out.

Sadd sat up and glared at me. ''You're back on that kick about somebody walking in on May! You promised me—''

''I didn't promise you anything. You asked me if I'd given up the thought and I said I supposed so. Well, I haven't.'' I stood up. ''And it wouldn't kill you to read Hen one chapter from an Oz book. You're not that sick.''

I went down the hall to Henry and Tina's room and

contemplated my wardrobe. I'd slept for most of the afternoon on their enormous bed after we'd quarantined Sadd, and Tina had gone out and bought me a pretty blouse to wear with what she called my "hunk of tweed."

I tried on the blouse and stared at it in the mirror. Better to say nothing to Peter Angier about Ellen this evening. I'd ask him to come visit Sadd tomorrow. Poor, sick Sadd would be so happy if an old friend were to drop by. How could an old friend refuse?

Pleased with myself, I started to brush my hair and my eyes dropped to a picture on the dresser top. I picked it up and swallowed hard. Henry Gamadge was stretched on the sofa of our living room on East Sixty-third Street and Henry Junior, perhaps three years old, was perched atop his father's bent knees. I was sitting on the floor beside them, infant Paula in my arms. My beloved Aunt Robby Vauregard, who had raised me, had wielded the camera, and it was Thanksgiving Day.

"Isn't that a great picture, Mom? Tina found it in one of the albums—aw, come on!"

I turned, sobbing wildly in my son's arms. Tina and Sadd apparently converged in the hall, took a look in, and withdrew. Henry hugged me rockingly and said:

"Remember that silly little rhyme he used to sing when he had me up on his knees like that? 'Trot, trot to Boston, Trot, trot to Lynn; watch the Mystic River or you might fall in!' And with 'IN,' down I'd go between his knees! How did Dad ever learn a nursery rhyme about Boston . . . ? You OK now?"

I nodded and kissed him and went back to brushing my hair.

"His parents always went to the Berkshires in the summer. What time should we leave to meet the Angiers?"

"Not for an hour or so. Hey, I have something nice to tell you. It seems Sadd notified the cemetery office that he wants to pay for Martin's slab to be inscribed. Father Dever just called to thank him."

"Oh, I am glad!"

"Something else, Mom."

His voice made me turn. Henry was looking at me with an expression I couldn't define. He went on:

"I got the impression, when we were talking with Sadd just now, that you think there was something fishy about May's death."

I sat down on the bed and just looked at him. Henry walked about the room as he talked.

"She certainly took her own overdose, we know that. But why? Why, when she was so hot to pursue the investigation? I haven't even said this to Tina, but would that anonymous letter really have blitzed May so badly? In fact, wouldn't it have had the opposite effect and egged her on?"

Oh, Henry Gamadge, you'd have been proud of this son!

I said: "Sadd wants no part of it. He thinks it's crazy. Maybe it is."

"Yes, maybe it is, and I think I'd let it go except for something that came in the mail this morning."

He took an envelope from his pocket and extracted a note and a check. The check was for twenty-five thousand dollars and was marked "gift." The note read: "Henry and Tina, you've been wonderful. This says thank you—May."

Henry said: "Her lawyer found it in her desk stamped and ready to mail."

I was overjoyed. "Henry, I couldn't be happier!"

"So if anybody did or said anything to make May destroy herself, I want to know who it was."

Tina put her head in the door. She saw the check in my hand and smiled happily. "Isn't that great?"

"Wonderfully great."

We walked downstairs and I told them my plan to invite Peter Angier to the house next day; they thought it inspired. Sadd's voice croaked after us that although he was dying he was also starving and who was going to bring him some supper?

The Othello was a low-key, very expensive Italian restaurant four blocks from Willow Street. The three of us walked there through a crystal clear night, and the Angiers were standing under the canopy. Ruth Angier, an angular woman about my age with a very nice smile, waved and said, "Bet these are the Gamadges," and Peter said, "Where's Sadd?"

It took till we'd checked our coats and been shown to a table to make explanations. Then Peter opened the wine list and said:

"I'm sorry Sadd is sick, but I'm kind of glad he's not here. I want to talk about Ellen Dawson."

Fortunately Ruth said something right away about ordering the wine and if we had no preference she'd like to recommend . . . and the three Gamadges sat nodding in dazed agreement.

Peter said, signaling to the waiter: "When I got that letter from Mrs. Dawson I felt sick, positively *sick*. To think of that poor woman sitting all alone in her apartment up on Park—and many's the time I've visited her there over the years because I felt so sorry for her— sitting there dreaming up this ghastly plan—well, I nearly called you two, but then the poor soul died and I assumed you'd dropped the thing, am I right?"

He gave the waiter an exotic-sounding wine order and

looked at Henry, who was drinking his water. Tina said, with admirable poise:

"Yes. We were distressed at the idea, too."

"I gathered so from what she'd said in her pitiful letter to me."

I thought—if he produces it, I'll scream. I can't look at another one. But he went on:

"Poor Mrs. Dawson. She mentioned you'd warned her it might prove painful—and futile. But apparently she was fond of you both, and trusted you, and was determined to go ahead."

Ruth said: "Not another word till we've ordered drinks." We got through that and then she said: "Here's where I'd give one thousand dollars for a cigarette."

We all commiserated and Peter said: "I'm proud of Ruth. It's been almost a year. In fact, I'm all-around proud of this lady. Did you know she was a distinguished journalist?"

Another chorus of admiration from the Gamadge gallery, and Ruth laughed and said: "Once you quit, who remembers? But I was fascinated by the Ellen Dawson story for years. I did an article on the fortieth anniversary of her disappearance in—let's see—that would have been in 1979. That's how Peter and I met. I interviewed him."

Our drinks arrived and I picked mine up eagerly. Henry said:

"It's easier to theorize about the case than it was to work on it. Given Mrs. Dawson's state of mind, we dreaded progress and dreaded nonprogress. Now we can go back to theory. What's yours, Mrs. Angier? Is Ellen dead?"

She smiled her nice smile. "I never had a theory. At least, I tried not to form one when I was writing the article. I wanted it to be a teaser: What do you think became of Ellen Dawson? It always seemed to me that the more interesting question was, why was she never found—dead *or* alive? Peter has a theory about that."

He picked up a menu. "For what it's worth. I think that in another time, even a decade before or after, Ellen's case would have been solved. God knows the Dawsons spent a fortune. But 1939 was a year with just one concern—war was coming, and Ellen got swallowed up in a great big priority." He handed me the menu. "What will it be, Mrs. Gamadge?"

"The scampi. I've heard its praises. Do you think Ellen is dead, Mr. Angier?"

"Of course she is. She was too fine a person to let those she loved suffer." He looked into space. "Ellen Dawson was one of those special women. . . . But, of course, you know this from Sadd. Oh my, oh my, I've never seen anybody so in love as he was."

Nothing could cover for us now. We simply stared at him, then at each other, speechless. Ruth said quickly:

"Peter, this isn't fair. They didn't know."

He looked from one to the other of us in dismay. "My God, I'm sorry. You didn't know that Sadd and Ellen were engaged? Secretly, of course."

Ruth said: "We're a pair of tactless boors. Let's drop the subject right now."

We all said no, please go on, in various dazed ways, and Peter said: "Well, we're going to get something inside us first," and the waiter took over.

Of course, of course, of course. Oh, my poor Sadd, how old would you have been when Ellen was eighteen? Twenty-five or -six and a cousin; was that why "secretly"? Oh, my dear, good friend . . . Peter had never seen anybody so in love as you. . . .

Peter was saying: "The summer before Ellen graduated, Sadd took a job in Boston to be near her, so her parents shipped her down to Patchogue to visit the Cavanaughs. He and Ellen were cousins and that seems to have been the principal objection, although Sadd felt that Mrs. Dawson had more exalted plans for her daughter. He had told me, just a few days before the prom, that he and Ellen were going to elope as soon as she graduated. So naturally my first thought when she disappeared that night was that they had. Eloped, I mean.''

And had they? I wondered dimly.

16

WE WALKED HOME IN ALMOST COMPLETE SIlence.

At one point Tina said "NO!"

"No, what?" said Henry. "No, Sadd didn't kill her, no, he doesn't know what happened to her, or no, they didn't elope?"

"All three."

"The first two anyway," I said.

"You'd think he'd have leveled with us before this." Henry took one of my arms and Tina took the other and we high-stepped through the slush at the corner of Willow Street. The light in the vestibule of Nice Ugly went on as we mounted the steps. The door opened and Sadd stood there, barefooted, bathrobe half on.

He said: "Tully's collapsed."

I thought—I may do the same. We stood in the hall listening. Just a few minutes ago a call had come from Paula in Boston. She'd said there was bad news—

"Stop right there," said Henry. He turned on a light in the living room. "Sit down, Mom. I'm going to get you a nightcap. Can't the details wait till morning, Sadd?"

"I suppose so," said Sadd huffily, "especially if Tully is already dead, in which case there's no—"

"In which case," said Tina, "that makes four: Lloyd,

123

May, Martin, and Tully. Where are your slippers, Sadd? Do you want to make five?''

He looked down at his feet. ''I guess they're next to my bed. I didn't bother with them when I answered the phone.''

''I'll get them.'' Tina went out, and I sat down on the sofa and accepted a cognac from Henry.

''Don't I get any?'' Sadd said wistfully.

I felt a pang as Henry poured another. I'd known Sadd only slightly in our youth. He'd been brilliant and funny, sturdy though not athletic, a little shorter than I. He'd married Harriet in his late thirties. She was chic, pleasant, colorless, and rich. I tried to imagine his young face alight with love. It was easy.

I said: ''I wonder who up there in Gloucester knew to call Paula.''

''Nobody. She called Tully. It seems you suggested she go visit him. When she phoned, a nurse answered. Tully had been poorly since his return from New York and had been seen in the garden in his shirtsleeves. The temperature up there being about thirty degrees, this was doing him no good. The neighbors decided to keep an eye on him. Thank you, Tina.'' She'd returned with the slippers.

I said: ''Thank God for neighbors.''

''This morning one of them knocked on his door and, receiving no answer, went in and found Tully in bed with a high fever. By the way, I think mine's down. I feel much—''

''Did they take him to the hospital?'' asked Henry.

''They wanted to, but Tully put up such a fight they simply called a doctor who sent in a nurse, and now Tully is somewhat worse and raving about having to tend his garden. Rather poignant, considering it's under two feet of snow.''

Tina said: "I guess that garden is his pride and joy. May said it was gorgeous."

"Oh, yes, that damn garden"—Sadd yawned—"one heard about it morning, noon, and night. You couldn't go there but he'd drag you around spouting the Latin name for everything. I remember once when I was visiting there in my youth—"

Sadd stopped, looking at us. Then he said:

"How was the dinner?"

"Super," said Tina.

"Great," said Henry.

"Full of surprises," said I.

"Such as?" said Sadd.

"Well, for one thing"—Henry poured himself a drink—"we learned that Peter's wife is an authority on Ellen's case. She was a journalist and met him when she was doing research on it."

Sadd looked genuinely astonished, then laughed. "And we were trying to think of tactful ways to broach the subject!" His face changed as we sat looking at him. "You said 'surprises.' Was there another?"

I said: "Yes, there was. The biggest one of all—for us."

Sadd pulled on his slippers and stood up reaching for the dangling cord of his bathrobe. He said:

"Now you know why I didn't join the party. May I have another cognac, Henry?"

I said: "Sadd, why didn't you tell us?"

"Because I couldn't bear to. Because it was all so long ago. Because it never had any bearing on the case. Peter was the only one I ever told. May knew Ellen and I loved each other, but she would have none of it. She claimed her objection was our being cousins, but I knew she wanted her daughter to make that brilliant match,

125

somebody rich and distinguished. As if 'rich and distinguished' meant anything to my precious girl.''

Can I bear this? I wondered. We sat like statues.

''We were going to be married in New York. Ellen said there would probably be a beach party after the dance, and she'd make some excuse to leave and walk back to the club—it wasn't far. I was waiting there in the car. Needless to say, I waited all night. End of story.'' He drained his cognac. ''You may believe it or not as you please.''

Tina was the first to move. She went to Sadd and kissed him.

I said: ''That goes for me, too.''

Henry said: ''Now the problem is what to do about Tully. Should somebody go up there?''

''I will,'' I said.

''We will,'' said Sadd.

''No, Sadd,''—I stood up—''you're going home.''

Rather to my surprise, he didn't object. We dispersed in silence, unusual for such a talky foursome.

I spent a completely wakeful night, grateful that I'd relegated myself to the divan in the dining room, for I wandered the first floor of the house for hours. Never had I understood so well the meaning of ''mixed emotions.'' I was filled with excitement at the thought of standing in the house where Ellen Dawson was last seen; I felt inexpressible pity for Sadd. I was exasperated with Tully—why couldn't he just go to a hospital and get himself taken care of—but I was grateful to him for this break. I sat at the living room window enjoying the sight of the dim, snowy street and the sound of the infrequent cars crunching by, but dreading the thought of more nights on a divan in a strange house. I sat in the kitchen doting on Hen's crayoned evocations of the Three Billy Goats, but was dismayed to think I'd probably have to spell Tully's nurse with trays. That sent me to the phone. I called the Parker House in Boston, an easy trip for Paula from her home in the South End. Tully would get me only as a commuter.

What time was it? Two-thirty and I hadn't closed my eyes. As I put the kettle on the stove, Loki woke sleepily out of the pantry. I made tea and sat holding him as I drank it. How wonderful that May had remembered Henry and Tina. I admitted to feeling a little jealous of her generosity to Jon and had secretly hoped . . . secretly engaged . . . Had May ever regretted her rejection of Sadd? Had she ever wondered if perhaps she'd have her daughter still if only—

I jumped—spilled tea on Loki's back—and he slid indignantly to the floor.

I hadn't asked Peter Angier if he'd been to see May. He'd spoken of "visiting her often over the years." When was his last visit? His wife's? How could he be so sure Ellen was dead? That she was "too fine a girl to cause her family suffering" was simplistic and it dismissed—perhaps intentionally—other appalling possibilities. Her case would have been solved, he'd said, in "another time."

I put out the kitchen light and went to bed, terribly wanting this to be Ellen's other time.

Tina woke me with the always ludicrous "Are you awake?" and I replied the always corny "No." She said:

"May's lawyer just called. He wants us to go to her apartment and get her clothes."

I'd been dreading this. "Why can't they just be sent to some thrift shop?"

"I told him you might want to do something like that,

but he wants us to come and 'make a selection.' It seems there's a mink coat and you might want it.''

"I don't. Do you?''

"No. He said he'd meet us there at ten.''

I slumped dejectedly back on the rumpled bedclothes. Tina looked at me. She said: "I could go alone.''

"Of course not.'' I staggered up. "Let me call Paula. What time is it? How's Sadd?''

"About nine. He's better but he still has a cold. There's Teresita.''

The kitchen door had opened, and Tina departed. I dressed and piled the bedclothes on a chair. I longed for my own bed, my own home. It was there waiting for me across the bridge. Perhaps Tina and I would walk past it after we left May's. I went to the phone and called Paula; I'd be on an afternoon shuttle to Boston and would go straight to the Parker House. Her joy warmed me.

And now, this was going to be the fastest sweep of a closet since Raffles.

I went into the kitchen and said: "Let's do the job in ten minutes and have lunch at the Colony.''

Tina said: "Yippee!''

We elected for the subway and a cab to "Seven-Forty" as May always called it. An impeccably dressed, elderly gentleman was waiting for us in the lobby. He introduced himself as George Lighter, and we rode up in the elevator. Mr. Lighter telling us about the estate sale that would transpire after "things were settled.'' As we walked into May's apartment, Tina said: "The picture's gone.''

Mr. Lighter said yes, it was being crated to be shipped to Mr. Hewitt in Massachusetts and did we know the sad story of the girl, and we said yes. He pulled open draperies, and I looked around the living room at the old, valuable—most of it—furniture, and the old, valuable—all of it—pictures and ornaments. I remembered the last time we had sat there, Henry Gamadge and I, talking to May. He had brought her a cribbage board for her birthday, and he said he'd teach her how to play and that would give him an excuse to visit her. Was there ever a kinder man—and Clara, if you dissolve once more you'll be the bore of the world.

Tina said: "Let's hit the closets."

We went into the bedroom. Mr. Lighter looked as if he thought it might be indelicate to follow, so I said:

"Won't you help us, please, Mr. Lighter? It's all just going to be piled into a cab and sent to the Salvation Army—unless you can suggest another place."

Mr. Lighter cleared his throat. "My daughter is in charge of the thrift shop at St. Clement's Church."

"Wonderful!"

Tina opened a closet and what seemed to be a hundred garments hung there. Happily, most were in plastic bags; May had always loved clothes and was meticulous about them. I started at one end and Tina at the other, and together we swept the lot onto the floor. Mr. Lighter gasped.

"Are you sure you ladies don't want—"

"We're sure." Tina was opening and closing handbags, turning out tissues, combs, cosmetics, and change. On the back of a chair lay the mink coat. I picked it up, thinking sadly that May had probably thrown it there when she returned from dinner with Tully at La Maison Bleue. It was, of course, magnificent, if you like that kind of magnificence.

I said: "Maybe this should go in the estate sale."

"Yes, I think it should," said Mr. Lighter, a little nervously.

I carried it into the living room and Tina called: "Be sure to go through the pockets."

They yielded one thing, a crumpled paper napkin from La Maison Bleue, though "crumpled" hardly described it; it was in shreds. It had been clawed and rent. There were spots of blood where the long nails May habitually wore had dug into her flesh.

Poor, poor lady.

Sadd was in a snit as I prepared to leave for the airport. "You've been prowling the streets of Manhattan, and now you're mad to get back. After all the effort I've put into your conversion to Florida, I find you dancing around the golden calf."

Henry said: "You'd better let her dance out to the car. The airport traffic will be brutal."

Sadd buttonholed me. "You're not to stay up there waiting for Tully to die or make a full recovery. Tina, make her promise to be back in Florida in a week."

"And back in New York in a month." Tina hugged me.

"Treacherous girl!" Sadd glared at her as I kissed him and told him to take care of himself. Hen asked to go to the airport with us.

"If you're in your duds in twenty seconds," said Henry, and I embraced Loki once more and we were off.

As we neared the expressway Henry reached into the backseat for a portfolio. He said: "Here's some in-flight reading. It's all the Ellen documents, including a copy of the anonymous letter. I kept the original. I have a plan of sorts."

"Fingerprinting?" I asked foolishly.

"Oh, Lord, no. We've all manhandled it beginning with May."

"What does 'manhandled' mean?" said Hen. He pronounced it so nearly perfectly that I had to hug him.

"It means what I'm doing to you now, love. What's the plan, Henry? Dear God, it's snowing again."

Henry put on the wipers. "Going on the theory that Ellen might be alive—because I don't buy Peter Angier's conviction she can't be—alive and able to write a letter or have it written for her, I thought I'd put a 'personal' notice in some of the papers. I'd use a few phrases from the letter, enough to indicate I have it, and suggest getting in touch with me regarding a mutual friend's will."

"Do you think"—I was a little stunned at the thought—"that she might not know May is dead?"

"Might not."

"But if one doesn't read the obituaries, is one likely to read the 'personals'?"

"Much more likely. Those things fascinate people."

I contemplated the sordidness of it. "So now there might be something in it for her. Or for her—her—"

"Keeper." He turned off at the airport exit.

"Henry, promise me you'll let Tina in on this."

"I already have. And Sadd's right, Mom—don't stay up in Gloucester too long. Tully doesn't have a whole lot of claim on you. I hope he's better, but whatever happens, Paula and I will take care of it between us."

The traffic at Departures was horrendous. I said: "Don't dream of parking. Dump me here. Darling Hen, let me manhandle you once more."

I boarded, clutching the portfolio, but in-flight reading gave way to a persistent in-flight thought. Sick or well, Tully was going to answer a question that had bothered me since leaving May's apartment: What cruel or blundering thing had he said to cause the pain that had shredded that paper napkin? They had talked about Ellen and, he claimed, May had been "calm."

Calm? Those fingers were convulsed.

17

THE OLD-FASHIONED, SEDATE LOBBY OF THE Parker House in Boston had blossomed, a few years ago, into a festive place for tea and drinks. From where I sat in a nook near the main door, the snow looked equally festive as it whirled down through the twilight of Tremont Street, and the pot of tea before me made the moment cosy, but the yellowing, eight-by-ten glossy photograph in my hand made it somber.

It was of Ellen Dawson in an evening dress. She was seated on a hassock, and the white folds billowed about her, accentuating her black hair. Pure Brenda Frazier, but more animated.

I looked at my watch, then at the door. Andy Fortina, Paula's husband, was, to use his own phrase, a "punctuality freak," while Paula struggled never to be more than half an hour late. Thus I calculated that Paula, coming from home, might make it in time to order dinner. Andy, coming from his office, would be here in three and a half minutes.

Three and a half minutes, then, to decide whether or not to involve them in the Ellen matter. Three and a half minutes to put the stuff spread before me on the tea table back in the portfolio or leave it out.

I took one of those minutes to pour a fresh cup of tea, eat a cucumber sandwich, and study Ellen's picture. I'd forgotten, or never realized, how tiny she was. I'd seen her once in our childhood and remembered a lively little girl who loved to play jacks. Aunt Robby and I had traveled to Boston for a family wedding, and at the reception, held in a house on Beacon Hill, Ellen and I had sat on the stairs like Beth and Amy peeking down at the party, consuming goodies, and playing jacks. She was skilled, I was klutzy, and I'd liked her.

Now, gazing at the pretty, merry face, I wished I'd known her. If she was still alive, how had she aged? Was that jet black hair as white as my own? Was she— oh, God—bent, mad, hostage?

"Who's that?" It was my son-in-law's voice behind me, two minutes early. Well, that settled it. As he kissed me, I said: "It's somebody I'll tell you about," and he sat down and let me pour him tea.

"I'll have my one precious drink before dinner. I plan to lose twenty pounds by the first of March." Andy always planned to lose twenty pounds by the first of something. He had what Evelyn Waugh called "a Latin love of bread."

"You look great, Clara. Florida agrees with you. What's in these microscopic sandwiches? Liver pâté—my favorite on earth." He picked up Ellen's picture. "This looks like an old movie photo." Andy worked for an education film company and was a thirties' movie buff. "Let's see . . . prettier than Janet Gaynor . . . not as pretty as Frances Drake . . . more like Maureen O'Sullivan but not so Irish . . . Jean Parker! She looks like Jean Parker."

Not unlike, I agreed.

"Who is it? Don't tell me." He sipped his tea and studied the photograph. "It's a glossy, so it was probably destined for the newspaper. If not an actress, maybe a debutante. That strapless white dress is definitely late thirties. . . ."

"Strapless? It can't be. Her parents would never have allowed it." I leaned over to look.

"You're right. Thin straps. Parents? Who is she?"

"Mother!"

I jumped up to hug Paula, only five minutes late.

"This is a miracle," said Andy. "You're not due for another hour."

"Don't be fresh." Paula sat down hanging onto my hand. "Mrs. Kelly came early and even offered to feed Janey. What's all this?" She looked at the array on the tea table.

Andy said; "This is called 'The Old Photo Game' or 'Who is She and Where is She Now?' "

"I don't know where she is now," Paula took Ellen's picture from his hand, "but I do know that her first name is Ellen."

I looked at her, stunned. "How do you know that?"

"This picture—a better copy—is in an album at Uncle Tully's house. It's signed 'Love, Ellen.' I went up to Gloucester to see him this morning." Paula sat down and reached for the teapot. "I called the nurse and she said he was fairly lucid—I guess he hadn't been—and a visitor might do him good, so Janey and I went up on the train—did she ever love that train!—and when we got there, the nurse was giving him a bath so we sat in the living room, and I looked around for something to read. The house is a *mess*. I found a bunch of old albums in one of the bookcases. So who is this? Wife? Daughter? Old girl friend?"

"Niece."

"Oh." A boring world. Paula promptly lost interest and poured herself tea, sternly inquiring of her husband if he was responsible for the empty sandwich plate, which he was. I ordered more, deciding that I still need not involve them. I started to gather up the documents, but Andy had picked up a clipping and was absorbed in it.

"Do you mean to tell me," he said slowly, "that this girl split from some dance back in 1939?"

"Yes."

"When did she show up again?"

"Never."

They looked at each other. Paula said, reaching for another clipping: "And she was Uncle Tully's niece?" She read the headline aloud. "HUNT FOR MISSING GIRL SPREADS TO OTHER NEW ENGLAND STATES. THE SEARCH FOR ELLEN DAWSON—she was related to you, too, Mom?"

I nodded. "Remember the old lady we used to take you and Henry to visit on Park Avenue—the one who just died?"

"Sure. Aunt May."

"Her daughter."

Andy said, staring at the picture: "And nobody knows what became of this kid?"

I shook my head.

"Or if she's alive or dead?"

I shook my head.

"How old would she be now?"

"About my age."

"Oh, she's got to be dead."

"Thank you."

We laughed, which helped. Andy said: "I only meant—after all these years . . . Was there ever a ransom demand?"

"Never."

Paula said: "I bet she eloped with some guy her family didn't like."

136

"They seem to think not." I quaked a bit.

"What a great movie." Andy closed his eyes. "She elopes with this guy—maybe he's married—and it doesn't work and she's too proud to go home. He leaves her and she dies—maybe kills herself—"

"No, I want it more upbeat," said Paula. "She marries again and lives happily but in obscurity—"

"—and that's her sitting over there with that poodle," I said.

"Where did you get all this stuff, Clara?" Andy poured himself more tea.

I hesitated, peering into the empty teapot. The anonymous letter, still safely tucked inside the portfolio, had been ticking in my head like a bomb. The ticking had begun that morning when Henry said he was going to try to contact the writer. Was this wise? Might it involve risk? Was it fair to extend that risk to Paula's family, who were even closer, geographically, to the fatal scene?

I stood up. "All this had been in May's apartment for years. I was asked to go there and collect her things." I swept everything together. "Now, listen: I'm going to take it all back upstairs to my room. Order more tea and I'll be right back. Then I want to hear about Tully and about Janey—"

Neither was listening. Andy held a police report with a map of the roads that led to Bass Rocks Beach. Paula began reading aloud, aghast: " 'Dear Sara: Forgive me for my silence of the last year but my heart is breaking and I must ask if you know anything that might help at this terrible time—' *Mom!*"

I sat down again.

It took through dinner and well into the evening to relate everything, withholding the anonymous letter and Sadd's involvement. At ten o'clock Andy rolled over on the bed in my sixth-floor room, holding a picture of the

Eastern Shores Yacht Club over his head. He studied it intently as Paula finished reading a synopsis of Tina and Henry's first visit to May's apartment. The lights of Boston glimmered through the snow now tapering off.

Andy said: "This club. I think my grandfather was the chef there once. Didn't it burn down?"

"Yes."

"He used to take me up there with him sometimes. We'd go to the beach, it was right near the club. I'll bet that was the same beach Ellen and her pals went to."

I thought of Sadd's words: "She'd make some excuse, it wasn't far."

Paula said: "What do Henry and Tina plan to do now that Aunt May is dead?"

"Their first inclination was to drop it but—"

"—but no way!" Andy laughed.

"What are you going to do, Mom?"

"I'm not sure."

"You are so." Paula is supposed to look like me, but her teasing smile is all Henry Gamadge. "You're going to do what Dad would have done—try to find out what happened to her."

I said firmly: "Well, I know what I'm going to do right now—I'm going to bed and you two are going home."

Paula said dreamily: "That Jim Cavanaugh. For my money, he's not in the clear. Oh, I know Ellen's not buried in that weirdo mausoleum—you told us what the guilty secret there was—but it doesn't mean he couldn't have been waiting for her that night."

Andy said with conviction: "There was a guy involved. There had to be."

I went to the closet for my nightgown. "May I remind you that you have a sitter? And I have to be on a train tomorrow morning."

138

"I brought you a timetable." Paula took it from her purse. "I don't know what poor Tully is like when he's well, but he sure is a skeleton now."

Depression settled on me. "He was always thin. What's actually wrong with him—pneumonia?"

"I guess so. The nurse didn't talk much, but she was nice. She took Janey out to the kitchen and gave her lunch. I don't think the poor guy knew who I was. He kept asking me, and I kept saying I was your daughter, and then he'd say, 'Dear Clara, dear Henry, how are they?'"

I cringed. "I dread this."

"Maybe you shouldn't go, Mom."

"Of course I should. It's what I came for."

"It's what used to be called, in my parochial school days, a 'corporal work of mercy.'" Andy reached for the portfolio and began gathering up the documents.

Paula said: "Do you want me to stay here with you tonight?"

"Certainly not. I want you on your way by the time I finish brushing my teeth."

I went into the bathroom, from where I could hear the murmur of their voices and the rustle of papers. Then there was a sudden silence and Andy said: "My God."

Still clutching my toothbrush, I looked out. They held the anonymous letter between them.

Paula said, looking pale: "It slid out when we opened the portfolio." Andy's hand, holding the letter, shook as he sat down.

I said resignedly: "Call Room Service. We're going to need sustenance for this."

The train that ran, and still runs, between Boston and the port city of Gloucester thirty miles to the north,

139

was one of the ways that Ellen Dawson could have conveyed herself—or been conveyed—into oblivion on that June night.

I thought of this as I looked out of the grimy train window at the snow-bordered bleakness of Boston Harbor, and the hour-long run to Gloucester began. The line, I'd been told by a venerable Parker House waiter at breakfast, used to be the Boston and Maine but was now part of the city transport system. He took it every day from his home in Lynn, and I was to try for one of the shiny new cars, where the heat came up better and the seats were more comfortable. I had, of course, been jostled into one of the old cars with a paucity of heat and cracked leather seats.

We slowed and stopped, and the train disgorged a swarm of students at what proclaimed itself as Bunker Hill Community College. I sighed with relief and put my purse and parcel on the seat beside me.

The parcel was a nuisance and an embarrassment. When I'd called Tully's nurse to say I'd be arriving on the eleven-forty train and would take a cab to the house, she'd asked me to please bring Mr. Hewitt another pair of pajamas. He had but one pair and it—she suppressed a giggle—was on its last legs. Really, I thought impatiently as I walked the few snowy blocks to Filene's, Tully couldn't be in such a state of penury. I felt a twinge of guilt at the familiar exasperation that always attended thoughts of Tully. I'd awakened in the middle of the night conscious that he probably could not talk rationally of his dinner with May, and my question regarding the conversation that had upset her would go unanswered.

The train stopped at Salem, and passengers poured on. A youth carrying an enormous skateboard paused beside me and gazed at purse and parcel. I transferred them to my lap and he sank down. I took the timetable from the purse and looked at the return trains. There was one at five-eighteen. That would give me about four hours to consult with the nurse, sit with Tully and remind him of who I was, and possibly get over to the Gloucester public library. Ruth Angier had said she'd written her article on Ellen ten years ago in the *New England Journal*. It was still a popular monthly, and I might find it in the back issues. I was curious to learn how Peter had answered her questions.

The skateboard tipped perilously toward me as its owner felt in his pocket for his ticket. The waiting conductor caught my eye and rolled his. He said: "Watch the lady with that thing," and I smiled a martyr's smile.

Gloucester at last. The depot was the usual dingy one in the usual dismal district of a fine, historic city. As I took the last, deep, ankle-breaking step from train to platform, I heard my name.

"Mrs. Gamadge?"

A woman my age in a red parka and well-worn slacks was walking toward me. A wool cap sat on her spiky gray hair, and her voice was hearty and pleasant.

"My name's Hester Connell—friend of Tully's. I thought you might like a ride over." My gratitude was so deep I could only gawk and smile. "I just talked to the nurse, and she said you'd be on this train. Here's the car—if it can still be called that."

I found my voice as she tucked me into the front seat of a dilapidated sedan, and I said it was the most beautiful car I'd ever seen, *ever*.

Hester laughed. "Know how you feel. Damn cabs are never around when you need 'em. What a trip for you. I understand you're all the way from Florida."

"Well, not today." I smiled. "How's Tully?"

"Bad. He can't make it. And this morning something

happened that nearly did him in. Do you mind if I stop here? Peggy—she's the nurse—asked me to bring her a quart of milk."

She was out of the car before I could ask what had nearly done Tully in. I sat staring at the sign over the grocery store in a kind of resigned stupor. Now she was back, and we lumbered into the traffic. Hester was quite a driver. She said: "You have to ride this thing like a buffalo."

"What happened to upset Tully this morning?"

"It seems some picture was delivered, a big thing all crated up, and when it arrived Tully was asleep. Peggy had it put on the back porch, and when he woke up he struggled out of bed to look out at his garden—he does this constantly, poor guy—and he saw the crate and wanted to know what it was, so Peggy—she's such a good soul—got a hammer and started to pull the slats off, and the first thing you know, Tully's passed out on the floor. She never got further than the top of the frame, so it couldn't have been the picture that threw him. Must have been the exertion."

18

HESTER BLEW HER APPALLING-SOUNDING horn at a refrigerator truck that blocked the main street. "Out of the way, fish," she muttered. I looked out at the crowded waters of the harbor, lifeblood of this city for three hundred years. Now we headed to the right of a sign that read: "Eastern Point, Scenic Route." Hester said:

"Tell me about yourself, Mrs. Gamadge. You related to Tully?"

"Not closely. But you know how it is at our stage. Not many of us left."

"Damn right. Plan to stay a while?"

"A few days if it helps."

"Rough weather for a Floridian."

"Oh, I'm a New Yorker. I've just been visiting in Florida. Have you always lived here?"

"Since year one."

"How long have you known Tully?"

"Ages. Knew his wife, Irene. Knew her sister, May Dawson. My parents had the house next to the Dawsons for years. The Hewitts were on one side, and we were on the other. Of course, they were summer people and we were year-rounders. My father sold most of the real estate along Bass Rocks."

"Did you know Ellen Dawson?"

"Sure did. You familiar with the story?"

"Yes."

"That business haunted me for years. Ellen was a few years younger than I was. She went to that ritzy private school, and I went to Gloucester High, so I only saw her in the summers, but she was a good kid—I liked her. My parents played bridge with Tully and Irene the night she disappeared. Have you had lunch? Want to stop someplace?"

"I don't want a thing." Except for you to keep talking, I wanted to add. We were passing a sign: ROCKY NECK, FIRST ART COLONY IN AMERICA. I said: "This place must teem in the summer."

"Teem is the word."

I made my voice reflective. "I've only visited Gloucester once before. My husband and I were on our way to Maine, and we stopped to see Tully. That was after May and Frank moved to New York. She just died, you know."

Hester nodded. "And not two weeks before that, I got a letter from her saying she was going to reopen Ellen's case. Of all the pathetic, misguided notions. I say it was a mercy she was taken."

We emerged from a winding road in a snow-packed, wooded area, and the Atlantic surged suddenly before us. I gasped.

"I'd forgotten how spectacular this is."

"Same old ocean." Hester turned down a broad road. "But most of the rest of it is totally changed. Look at that motel—right out of Atlantic City. And a lot of the big old places—ours included—are guest houses."

"You don't live here now?"

"No. When my father died in 1960, my mother and I bought a house in Rockport, next town over. I taught school there for years. Never married. Here we are."

144

Hester turned into an unplowed driveway and gunned her way to the middle of it. "By the way, where are you staying? Not here with Tully, I hope. You couldn't stand it."

I looked up at the great, old weatherbeaten house, a single attic shutter flapping, and said thankfully: "I'm at the Parker House."

"In Boston?" Hester looked horrified. "You'll be *dead* going back and forth. Glad to have you stay with me—ten minutes from here."

"I wouldn't dream of it, Miss Connell. You've already been so kind—"

"Talk about it later. This your package? Where's that damn milk? Watch your door—it tends to fall off."

Hester must have been a wonderful teacher. I felt shepherded, secure, informed, instructed—and tempted to accept her invitation. *Her parents had played bridge with Tully and Irene the night Ellen disappeared.* In the words of the song, Hester if ever I should leave you . . . it wouldn't be tonight.

She was right about the car door. The wind whipping in from the ocean sent it crashing back against the hood. Hester came around saying, "Let me do it," and heaved it back in place. We were blown up the ten steps to the porch, which was empty and snow-drifted. I had a fleeting vision of tea trays, long shadows, wicker furniture, and Mah-Jongg. The front door opened, and a young and pretty nurse greeted us.

Hester said: "This is Mrs. Gamadge, Peggy."

"Gee, your daughter looks just like you." Peggy won my heart at once. She accepted the milk. "Thank you, Miss Connell. Mr. Hewitt isn't too good. He had that fall, you know. I'll be right back—his lunch is on the stove."

She disappeared. Hester put our coats on a tipsy rack

that stood more or less in the middle of the hall. Closed double doors on our right led, I assumed, to the bedroom (converted from dining room). We walked into the living room, which was inexpressibly dreary. The general impression was one of disorder, neglect, and lifelessness. Curtains hung stiff with grime, the rug gave off little puffs of dust at each footstep, and the furniture stood about in no particular order, appearing to have been shoved here and there for a passing purpose and never replaced. A handsome knee-hole desk bore a jumble of papers, a gooseneck lamp, and an ancient typewriter; business of sorts was apparently conducted here. A card table near the window was piled with magazines and newspapers. I glimpsed a corner of the faded felt cover painted with spades and clubs. Possibly the very table that seated the players who played the game that covered the hours that saw the tragedy that Jack built.

Hester said: "Ghastly, isn't it. Look here."

She took an open checkbook from the desk and held it out to me, saying: "I didn't pry. Peggy showed it to me. We're old friends—I taught her in the eighth grade."

The checkbook was the kind with three checks to a page. Not more than ten had been written, but as Hester flicked the pages I saw that dozens had been signed. A treasurer's nightmare.

I said: "Is he mad?"

"In this case, not so mad as you'd think." Hester closed the checkbook and found a seat for herself on the edge of a bentwood chair piled with seed catalogues. "Peggy told me that the first day she came, Tully, who was still fairly *compos mentis*, asked her to bring him the checkbook and sat up in bed signing all those checks. He told her she was to pay herself any salary she wanted, pay the doctor, pay any bills that came in, and this way he'd be certain of not being taken to the hospital.''

I said: "Carte blanche if she'd just keep him here?"

Hester nodded. "He's just lucky she's an honest girl.'' She stood up and looked around. "I wonder where Tully keeps his booze? Irene always had some in that breakfront.''

Peggy came in with a bottle of wine and two glasses. "Have you ladies had lunch? I can fix—''

"You have a fix right there, Peggy, thank you.'' Hester took the wine from her. "But do you mind if we sit in the kitchen? This room gives me the creeps.''

"Sit at the kitchen table, Miss Connell, and make yourselves sandwiches. There's ham in the fridge. I'm going to see if he's awake.''

The kitchen showed signs of recent sprucing, antiquated though everything was. Peggy had obviously done some clearing and scrubbing, and I was grateful for the sandwich Hester made. What a cheerful spot it must have been once, with the blue Atlantic always performing for you as you stood at the sink.

"Now, look,'' Hester sat opposite me at the table, "you can't pile back and forth on that train. Stay with me and give it three days. Then, if Tully is still with us, I'll handle it till the end.''

"Miss Connell—''

"Hester.''

"Hester, you are what my children would call a 'neat lady.' I just wish Tully knew how fortunate he is—''

"Oh, bosh. Other people are in and out, too.''

"But you're special. I know you're that special one.''

"I'm the oldest one, that's for sure. Nobody along here remembers as far back as I do. Tully and I could always talk.''

147

I said: "How old is he? I never did know."

"Let's see . . ." Hester slathered more mustard on her sandwich. "He was younger than Irene—I remember she used to joke about it—and she was my parents' age. I guess he's middle to late eighties. Of course, they both aged badly after the Ellen thing."

I sipped my wine. "What do you think happened that night?"

"Well, I know one thing that happened: Those four kids were someplace else besides Bass Rocks Beach—whoops—here's a napkin."

The jerk of my hand which splashed the wine down my front was mild compared to the leap of my mind. *Someplace else besides Bass Rocks Beach.* Now Peggy was back, her step brisk.

"Mr. Hewitt's awake and heard voices and said he wants to see you."

Hester stood up. "Take Mrs. Gamadge in, Peggy. I'll bring his tray."

As we walked through the living room, I said: "Did you tell him my name, Peggy?"

"Yes, I did. He said, 'Oh, isn't that nice, I thought she was in Florida.' He's quite clear at the moment, but he goes in and out."

"He's lucky to have you. I brought the pajamas."

"Yes, thank you, I saw them. I put them on him. Remind me to give you a check."

With troopers like Peggy and Hester on hand, Tully's condition was now the least of my worries. My one desire was to find a quiet table for dinner and pump Hester on "someplace else besides Bass Rocks Beach."

Peggy opened the double doors, and I prepared my smile, but it was hard to maintain at the sight of poor Tully, pitifully changed in the mere few days since I'd seen him. He looked like a scarecrow in his new blue pajamas, and they were the only bright spot in the room. He held out his arms to me and said, as I embraced him:

"Clara, I did such a dumb thing. Why didn't May tell me she was sending Ellen's picture?" His breath came in little gasps. "When I saw that frame I could have been back in May's living room. I'm afraid I— what do the kids say—'freaked out.' "

"You certainly did." I kept smiling. "But that black-and-blue spot on your forehead goes nicely with your new pajamas."

Peggy had pulled up a chair for me, one of the old dining room set of which half a dozen still stood about. She went out and I said:

"Weren't you smart to make this into a bedroom." I refrained from adding that he might have removed such cumbersome items as sideboard and table, which he had merely jammed into a corner. Tully looked as if he were ensconced in a used furniture shop. "By the way, your nice friend, Hester Connell, picked me up at the station. She's a dear."

"Yes, isn't she." Tully looked at me with a clear and intelligent gaze. "Did Henry come with you?"

It wasn't possible. I hesitated, then said: "No, he and Tina couldn't get away. They sent their love."

"I mean your husband."

I supposed I'd heard that a mind could become compartmentalized, but it was still a shock. I said: "Tully, Henry's dead."

"Oh, I'm sorry to hear that." He looked distressed, then added: "I lost Irene, too, you know. And May died recently. She had Ellen's picture sent to me—did I tell you? I'm afraid I wasn't expecting it. That's how I got this bruise." The poor creature looked at me in perplexity. "I don't understand this. My health has al-

149

ways been so good. I just said to May this morning that I was fine until she said she was going to look for Ellen. I'm sure that's what upset me.'' Now he smiled brightly. ''Did you say Hester brought you? Is she still here?''

''She sure is.'' Hester's voice at the door was a comfort. ''And she's got a tray of lunch you're to eat right now.''

She yanked one of the chairs forward with her foot and sat down beside me. ''Pull your sheet over the blanket, Tully. Not that lunch can do much harm to it. Good God, did this bedding come from the Ark?''

''I don't want any lunch.'' Tully slid down on his pillows and looked into space. ''I want to go out to my garden.''

Hester and I sat there not looking at each other. Then she said:

''If you don't eat you'll never go out there again. You won't have the strength.''

Tully lay with his eyes closed, breathing shallowly. Hester shrugged and we stood up. His eyes opened and he smiled at me.

''Clara, you were so nice to come. Bring Henry next time.''

As Hester and I walked to the door, she took a piece of bread from the tray and munched on it. In the living room Peggy was on the telephone, and I heard the word ''oxygen.''

''Good thing, too.'' Hester put the tray on the pile of seed catalogues. ''The portable stuff, Peggy?''

''Yes.'' Peggy hung up. ''He wouldn't use it last time I ordered it. Now he has no choice. Do you have the sales slip for the pajamas, Mrs. Gamadge?''

''Oh, please.'' My depression deepened. ''Consider it a gift.''

I walked to the big window that overlooked the garden, vaguely remembering that the ocean fore and the garden aft had made the place spectacular. Now, with only posts here and there to define paths, the garden lay sleeping under the snow. The two beautiful spruce trees that stood at one end, a stone bench between them, were bowed and white.

My eye traveled to a corner of the kitchen porch where a large box leaned against the railing.

I said: "Hester, we'd better get that crate inside or the portrait will be ruined. It's Ellen, you know."

"It's *what*?" Hester, who'd been sipping Tully's soup, walked to the window.

"It's a portrait of Ellen when she was a child. It always hung in her parents' home. He recognized the frame."

"For pity's sake. So that's what did it. What shall we do with it?" She looked around. "One more thing in here, and we can rent the place out for a horror movie."

I said: "I think we should hang it."

"*Hang* it? My God, if the frame alone sent him into a tailspin . . . Of course, poor Tully will probably never come in this room again—but"—she gazed at the walls—"where?"

"Right there." I pointed to where a scattering of family pictures hung tipsily. "It belongs here. This house was as much Ellen's home as the one next door."

"True enough."

"I'll pay somebody tomorrow to come put it up." I felt a sort of elation. Ellen was home again.

"Hester, I'm going to take you up on your offer to stay with you."

"I'm delighted, Mrs. Gamadge."

"Clara."

19

I HAD NEVER BEEN IN THE SEASIDE TOWN OF Rockport, which, Hester told me, suffered being described variously as "arty," "charming," and "picturesque."

It could have been all those things as far as I was concerned. My preoccupation, as we sat that evening in a nice restaurant overlooking the town beach, was whether or not to level with Hester. Would my questions regarding Ellen be purposeful or academic? I decided on the latter as Hester read aloud from the menu, recommended the swordfish, and ordered it. This was a family matter. I wanted to do what my husband had always done, go quietly about my investigations and keep them to myself or even abandon them. What Henry and Tina did in New York was their business and their right. But here, where the story had happened and was still open-ended, I felt a distaste, even a dread, of making my intentions known.

Hester produced a bottle of wine from a paper bag. "Welcome to the quaint customs of a dry town. You can't buy it here, but you can bring it. Shades of Hannah Jumper."

"Who's she?"

"Big temperance lady back in the nineteenth century. Got all the Rockport women out with axes to smash the rum kegs and the town's been dry ever since. Of course, the amount of liquor consumed here would fill a quarry—and that reminds me to answer your question about Ellen Dawson.''

I was afraid she'd forgotten it, and I didn't want to appear to press. ''What question? Oh, yes, about where she'd been that night other than the beach.''

''She'd been at the quarry. Flat Ledge Quarry. All those kids had.''

I repeated blankly: ''The quarry. Flat Ledge Quarry.''

''Take you there after dinner if you like.'' Hester popped the cork and filled our glasses. ''All the young people, including me, used to swim in the quarries. Kids still do. It's forbidden, of course, and risky as hell, but fun—especially at night. Especially Flat Ledge. Try the wine.''

I did, grateful not to have to speak for a few seconds. Then I said: ''Delicious. Nice and dry. How do you know she was there?''

''Saw her.''

I took another sip and laughed a little laugh. ''Now, Hester, you've thoroughly aroused my curiosity. No fair stopping there.''

''OK. A short lecture first—it's the schoolteacher in me.'' Hester put her elbows on the table, her wineglass in both hands. ''One of the early industries of this town was quarrying. A quarry is what they call 'working' until the blasters hit water. For years, even decades, they blast and blast, and then one day spring water gushes up, and that's the end of that one. There haven't been any working quarries in Rockport for over fifty years. They're all filled with lovely spring water. Some of them have even become private swimming clubs. They're very deep and very dangerous.''

153

"Sounds exotic."

"I used to have my kids in school write an essay on the place in Rockport they liked best." Hester smiled into her wine. "A bright little girl once wrote, 'At night the quarry looks like a scene from *The Arabian Nights*.' Judy, you're a wonder. We're starving."

The waitress put steaming plates before us and said: "I told Kenny to give you and your friend 'specially nice pieces, Miss Connell."

"Kenny still here? I thought he went in the Navy. This is Mrs. Gamadge—Judy Purcell—had her in school."

I smiled at Judy, wondering if there was anybody in town Hester hadn't had in school.

"He's going next week," said Judy. "I'll get your rolls."

I said: "Hester, I've read practically every account of the night Ellen Dawson disappeared. Nowhere have I seen anything about a quarry."

"Of course you haven't. Because I promised her. Tell you about it when we go up there. Right now we should settle something about Tully: He's going to need a third nurse. There's Peggy, and one at night, and I've been taking the early morning shift—"

"Hester, you haven't!" I laid down my fork in dismay.

"It hasn't killed me—it's only been for the last two days—but I can't keep it up, I'm too old. Besides—I'll be honest—I don't want to be there when the poor guy dies. Will you authorize the expense for the third nurse?"

"I thought he authorized all expenses himself."

"Yes, but are his funds without limit? Suppose the checkbook runs out. Do you know anything about his finances?"

"Nothing." I felt inadequate in the face of Hester's competence. Dragging my thoughts from quarries, I added, "I'll talk to his lawyer tomorrow. Do you know who it is?"

"Sam Venner. Same as mine."

I became brisk. "One thing is certain—tomorrow *I* take the early shift."

"Nonsense—"

"And the minute I finish this fabulous swordfish, I'm going to the phone to call my daughter. Thanks to you, she can cancel my room at the Parker House. And I don't want to hear another word about tomorrow morning. I truly want to do it. What time does the night nurse leave?"

"Don't gag. Five A.M."

I gagged.

Rockport did indeed look "picturesque" in the snowy winter dusk as we walked back to Hester's snug, clapboard house on a hilly side street. Her monstrous car stood in the driveway.

"Hop in," said Hester, "and we'll go quarrying."

"I can't wait." I never meant anything more. "How many quarries are there?"

"Half a dozen or more. Some big, some little. Flat Ledge is the most spectacular, to my mind."

"That's where Ellen was swimming."

"Hold on—I didn't say *she* was swimming." Hester backed out of the driveway and into a snowbank. "Damn." She pitched out of it. "This is a one-way street, thank heaven."

Thank heaven indeed. We more or less careened down it and onto Main Street.

"How far?" I asked.

"Less than a mile."

155

Less than a mile from these guest houses and gift shops to something worthy of *The Arabian Nights*? We skirted a beach and went up an incline past a row of undistinguished houses to a stone bridge. Hester pulled in tight against the bordering snow.

"I'll put my blinkers on, but we can't stay long, nothing can pass us. If you suffer from vertigo don't go farther than the bridge. Let's move."

I clambered from the car, she took my arm, and we walked across the frozen street to the bridge and looked over.

A meteorite, rather than men, might have made it. A half-mile wide? Jagged, sheer, snow-etched granite sides plunged to a pool of black water at the bottom. An early moon trembled there. How deep? I must have murmured the last aloud.

"God knows," said Hester. "More damn drownings in these places. But you can imagine how thrilling to splash around down there."

"You said Ellen wasn't swimming."

"No. Blast this snow. It's hard to envision what happened on a summer night fifty years ago. We'd better get back in the car. I think I hear the snow plow."

We drove across the bridge, and Hester pulled into somebody's driveway. The plow rumbled by, and she pulled out again. We moved slowly back across the bridge.

"See that fence? The old one was flimsier. We used to crawl under it and slip and slide down the rocks, they're not as sheer on this side. That stone building"— it loomed across the bridge—"was the only one here. It was the old quarry office. There wasn't much else but fields between here and the ocean."

I leaned out of the car window, straining for a glimpse

of the drop. "Where was Ellen?" I knew my voice was urgent. "Where did you see her?"

Hester's voice grew husky. Was she caught up in the memory?

"Right there. She'd just cleared the rocks and was running across the grass bank in that gorgeous white dress, holding it up so she wouldn't trip. It was bright moonlight and I heard her laughing. I was coming across the bridge—just as we are now—in my father's car. I'd been baby-sitting up in Pigeon Cove. I slowed down and called out, 'Ellen, is that you?' and she wriggled under the fence and ran to the car and said, 'Oh, Hester, I'm so glad it's you—you won't snitch.' Then I could see the other kids coming up, two boys and the other girl, and the boys were in their underwear and carrying their evening clothes, and the girl was in her prom dress, and they were all laughing fit to kill. Ellen called them over to the car and introduced me."

Hester had stopped in the middle of the bridge. Please God, don't let another car come.

"I wasn't much older than they were, but I was a senior in college and felt grown-up and important, so I lectured them on how dangerous, et cetera, and Ellen's date—the poor boy died in the war—said it was all his fault; he'd heard about the quarries and always wanted to swim there."

The car stalled. Hester started it up again and moved forward.

"Then I asked if they needed a lift, and the other boy, Peter Somebody—I forget his last name—said no, that was his car over there, and the other girl said she felt cheated because she hadn't had a swim, and Ellen said—I remember this distinctly: 'Let's go to Bass Rocks Beach, it's near my house, and I'll go home and get suits for us both.'"

157

I said: "That fits with the record."

"That fits with the truth. I followed Peter's car back to the beach and saw them all pile out. I started to drive on and then I heard Ellen calling—oh, God, I can hear her now—and I stopped and she ran up to the car window and leaned in and hugged me and said: 'Promise me you won't tell on them.' It wasn't till later I remembered she'd said 'them.' You won't tell on *them*—not *us*. That's when I realized she must have been planning not to be around. It could never be proved that she went off with anybody, but I always believed she had."

We were back on Hester's street. The trip had taken fifteen minutes and fifty years. She pulled into her driveway and turned off the ignition. We sat in silence. Then Hester said:

"I always wish I'd gone back to my parents' house that night. I might have seen Ellen when she left the beach. But it was Saturday, and I had a final exam on Monday, so I drove back to my dorm at Salem State."

I was cold, but I dreaded moving. I said: "You said something about a bridge game, your parents and the Hewitts."

"Yes, but that broke up around midnight, and it was already past two when I left the kids at Bass Rocks Beach. My mother said Tully woke them up about five, white as a sheet. He'd waited up—Irene had gone to bed—and when Ellen didn't come in by four he'd driven all around town looking for her. He hadn't had the courage to wake Irene up—let alone the Dawsons. My mom and dad went over there with him, and they called the police. Beginning of trail." Hester turned off the car lights, and we sat in darkness. "And end of trail." She jumped. "I think I hear the phone."

She was out of the car and up the steps to her back

door. I followed, dazed. Hester extended the receiver to me as I walked into the kitchen.

"For you. Your son in New York. He sounds nice."

She went outside again, and I heard the garage door open. I said: "Henry, how did you ever—oh, of course, Paula."

He said: "I'm working on the 'personal' for the papers. Can I read it to you? You may have a suggestion."

"I do, dear. Don't run it. Ellen's dead."

20

HALF AN HOUR LATER HESTER AND I WERE sitting in our "wrappers" (she howled when I used the term—shades of her grandmother!) having hot chocolate and deciding that to expect the single taxi in Rockport to come for me at four-thirty A.M. was futile.

I said: "A lot of relief I am to you if you have to drive me to Tully's at that hour."

"I don't mind. I'll come home and go to bed again." She looked at me steadily. "Your son's call has upset you."

I was grateful she thought it was that. Was it so evident my heart was pounding? I stood up. "He wants me to come home tomorrow. I may, if you can get that other nurse."

"Oh, I can get her. I just hate to lose you."

I put my arms around her, wanting to weep. "Hester, I'll never forget you."

"What kind of talk is that? You won't have the chance. I may turn up on your doorstep if you don't promise to come back."

"I'm going to count on that."

"Go to bed now. You're beat. I'll set my alarm."

I had a ghastly thought as I beamed my borrowed flashlight on Tully's steps and Hester roared away in the darkness. That oxygen. How did it work? What did one do? Might Tully expire gasping because of my inefficiency? It was my first nervous question to the nurse when she opened the door. The good soul was all reassurance.

"Mr. Hewitt knows how to use it. It's right by the bed. He's asleep now. He's been awful restless all night."

She was middle-aged, sleepy, and ready to leave. I would be too, I thought, watching her button her coat. The house was unaired and oppressive, lighted only by the glare of the television that was yapping away in a corner of the living room.

"Well, I'm on my way. The doctor's number is right by the phone. There's coffee on the stove."

I offered my flashlight, but she was down the steps and in her car with all the nimbleness of release. Tires crunched on the snow, and I was alone with Tully.

The first thing I did was to turn off the television. Silence except for the sea, blackness except for a predawn glimmer. My flashlight showed me the desk. I went to it, turned on the gooseneck lamp, took a piece of paper from the jumble, and rolled it into the ancient Remington. Standing there with shaking knees, I typed: Do not, I beg you, pursue the investigation of your daughter's disappearance. It was enough. I hardly needed to take the letter from my handbag. The faded type, the clogged "u," the tipsy "v," all sickeningly the same.

I pulled the paper from the machine and sat down to steady myself. Was I going to be sick? Would my legs hold me when I stood up again? The phone rang.

Why does that sound, of all sounds on earth, have the power to galvanize the most inert of us? I got myself into the kitchen and took the receiver from the wall. It was Hester.

"As I walked into my house the phone was ringing. It was your son. He's on his way here."

"Here?" I think I said.

"I was to tell you that he left home around midnight. Neither he nor his wife could sleep after he talked to you. The drive takes about six hours and he was calling from Boston, so he should be at Tully's in half an hour or so. I gave him directions. I hope he's not in any trouble, Clara. None of my business, of course."

I said, my heart lifting within me: "No, Hester. It's just a—a family matter I'm helping settle. Thanks so much for letting me know."

"How's Tully?"

"Asleep."

"Call me if you need me."

"I will."

Light was coming in from the sea. Henry was on his way. Now I had the courage. I walked across the hall and opened the double door. Tully was sitting up on one elbow. He said, gasping:

"What time is it?"

"Almost six, Tully."

"I have to let Irene know. I can't wait any longer."

I walked to the foot of the bed. "Tell me something first. Did Ellen know you were in love with her?"

He dropped back on the pillow. "Not till just now."

"When she came in?"

"She didn't come in—that's the trouble! She went around to the garden, and I saw her take the suitcase from behind the spruce tree."

"And you went out and tried to stop her?"

"Of course I did. Somebody had to." He was motionless, staring at the ceiling. "I told her how bad her

162

parents would feel, and she kept saying she was sorry, but she loved Sadd and that was that. I told her how bad *I'd* feel''—he began to tremble so violently that the bed shook—''and she put her arms around me and said she knew how much I loved her, and I said, *'No you don't, you don't know the half of how I love you!'* ''

Terrible sobs now, choking sobs. I got the prongs of the oxygen into his hands, and he never stopped talking while I sat on the bed, numb.

''When she began to cry and shake and pull away, I had to stop her, keep her quiet. I was afraid she'd run into the house or next door. I kept telling her I'd never say these things to her again, but she was hysterical.''

Tully was fast becoming the same. I said: ''Tully, it's over. I'm going to get you a brandy.''

''It isn't over! Those other kids were here just now asking where Ellen was and why she hadn't come back to the beach. I've been out in the car pretending to look for her! Now, I have to tell Irene and May that Ellen never came home and then—''

''Not just yet, Tully.'' He was struggling to get out of bed. Oh, Henry, come, come. ''Not till you've had a brandy. That will help—you know a brandy will help you tell—now, won't it?''

''Yes.''

I pressed the wretched, shaking form back into the bed and prayed, as I backed toward the door, that he would stay there. He did, breathing raspily. The final, dreadful question had to be asked, and I needed brandy myself to ask it. But would this vivid replay last? Would Tully smile at me when I returned and ask how Henry was?

The breakfront. Hester had said Irene kept it in the breakfront. Sure enough, there was the stash. Now the kitchen for glasses—cups—anything—and I was back across the hall, but not soon enough.

Tully was gone.

Standing there staring at the empty bed, I'm ashamed to confess that the first thing I did was pour myself a quick one. Nothing that happened now could be one-tenth as terrible as what happened on that June night. Tully had come full circle, and I knew where to look for him.

A car door slammed, and I went into the hall and out to the porch. Henry was up the steps two at a time.

I said: "Not here. In the garden."

He took my arm and we plowed through the snow around to the back of the house. It was quite light now, and the two big spruce trees on either side of the stone bench were glistening and beautiful. Tully knelt beside the bench, his head resting on it, his arms embracing it.

I said: "It was the only headstone he could give her."

"It was Hester," I said. "Hester said the words."

Andy said: "But you *heard* them."

We were in the same nook in the Parker House lobby, and Henry was with us this time. Andy was again making short work of the sandwiches, and Paula had just arrived breathlessly.

Henry said: "How many times—dozens, maybe hundreds of times—was it reported that Ellen Dawson's aunt and uncle had 'waited up'? The fact that one of them had gone to bed and the other had done the waiting probably wouldn't have meant that much anyway."

"Until you do what your father called 'worry it.' " I looked at my watch; my plane to Sarasota was in fifty minutes. "I'm sure a lot of people believed with Hester that Ellen had planned to 'go off' with somebody—

Paula and Andy insisted there was a man involved—but we had the advantage of knowing who it was and that we trusted him. I was pretty sure she'd take a bag of some sort—at least something to change to from her prom dress—and that probably meant a return to the house, or at least the grounds. Between there and Sadd was only . . . Tully.''

Mention of Sadd's name affected us all similarly. We drank our tea in silence, then Paula said:

"Will you tell him?"

"Never," I said instantly. "Nor anyone else. It ends with the five of us—I'm including Tina, of course. I hope we agree on that?"

They nodded, and Andy said, with his mouth full:

"When do you figure Tully mailed the letter?"

"When he came down for Lloyd's funeral," said Henry. "He'd come a day earlier. He'd gotten his letter from May like all the rest a few weeks before. When May said she was going ahead anyway, he probably hit her with the truth, and that did her in."

I said: "Something Tully himself said the night of Lloyd's wake stuck in my mind. We were wondering if there'd be people who'd remember Ellen when they learned of May's death."

Henry snapped his fingers and sat forward. "And Tully said fifty-year-old *crimes* tend to be forgotten."

I said: "Sadd said 'this wasn't a crime, it was a disappearance—' "

We recited together " 'it isn't a crime to disappear.' "

Henry and I beamed at each other, Andy applauded gently, and Paula poured herself tea with an odd expression. She said:

"Just before I left home I got a phone call. It was Hester. I'm supposed to ask you something, Mom."

We looked at her expectantly. She looked back over the rim of her cup with her father's eyes.

"That darling, innocent lady . . . wanted to know . . . if we thought it would be nice . . . if Tully's ashes were to be sprinkled in his garden. He loved it so."